An Ambassador's Ploy

Praise for
The Adventures in Eldnaire Trilogy

"The title pulls us in. The authentically conflicted protagonist holds us there. The twists and knots of her journey won't let us go. And we hope they won't! We're caught in your grip, Thirzah. What do you have for us next?"

Nancy Rue

Award-winning author of *The Lily Series*

"A debut novel filled with romance, sibling rivalry, and the difficult decisions of staying true to oneself."

Kim Catron

#1 Bestselling Author of *Threshing of Straw*

"This enchanting story drew me in and had me turning pages right to the end. The characters were a delight to get to know."

Rebekah Olson

Author of *Spell Caster*

"An amazing young adult fantasy novel! *The Adventures in Eldnaire Trilogy* is a great adventure, and Thirzah is a new author to watch!"

Brad Pauquette

Author of *Sejal: The Walk for Water*

An Ambassador's Ploy

Adventures in Eldnaire
Book Three

Thirzah

The Pearl

PEARLBOOKS.CO

Developmental Editor
BRAD PAUQUETTE

Copy Editor
VELLA KARMAN

Book Designer
ALLI PRINCE

LCCN: 2025945285

Print ISBN: 978-1-960230-18-8
E-book ISBN: 978-1-960230-19-5

This book is dedicated to everyone who wished they could grab me by the shoulders and shake me as hard as they could after they reached the end of the second book.

Please accept this third and final book in the trilogy as my apology.

And to my brother, who, in case you were wondering, *still* has not read any of the other books I've dedicated to him.

One

My heart thumped within my chest like a fist knocking at a wooden door. Air escaped my mouth through shaky breaths. Mice skittered across the stone floor somewhere outside of my cell, and the crystal torches on either side of the door to the outer room hummed.

My nose had grown used to the smell of wet cement, rust, and urine by now. I sat in the center of the cell, hugging my knees close to my chest. Tears blurred my eyes.

It couldn't have been more than ten or twenty minutes since Sir Fern had left the room, but it felt like it had been days since I had seen another human being. My ears strained to hear the sound of guards approaching, of Sadie being brought back safe and well.

Instead, my ears picked up faint voices coming from beyond the barred window just below the cell's ceiling.

I reached a hand up to wipe away the tears obscuring my

vision, but stopped short, allowing them to drop. What did it matter? There was nothing in the cell that was worth seeing clearly, and by this time I had memorized each nicked and rusty spot on the bars. Even with my eyes closed I could picture the soiled straw covering the stone floor I sat on, the thirty-seven tally marks scratched into the walls by a previous prisoner, and even the small cracks in the ceiling.

Thanks to the floor-to-ceiling horizontal and vertical iron bars of my cell—hardly big enough for me to reach out of—there would be no escaping or leaving the dungeon. At least, not before my execution.

An icy shiver snaked its way up my spine, and I hugged my knees even tighter. Anger and regret clawed at my mind like a wild animal, tearing my last thoughts of hope to shreds.

Listening to my brother Leon, trusting Sir Fern, and returning to Vilnaria had turned out to be the *worst* decisions I had ever made in my entire life. Now, Sadie was gone, I was about to be executed, and Vilnaria was closer than ever to going to war against Myarna—my homeland. And worse still, there was *nothing* I could do about any of it.

Sir Fern had said Emperor Kyvir wouldn't interfere with his plans to execute us—but what did that mean? Was Kyvir sitting somewhere in the palace just as trapped as I was? What if Sir Fern had harmed him?

My arms, legs, and back were beginning to ache, and my chest was sore where my knees were digging into it. But what did it matter? What did anything matter anymore? After all, I would be executed in the morning.

I waited for what felt like hours before I finally fell asleep, but Sadie never returned to our cell. When the door to the outer room did open, it was just a guard with another plate of food—and no matter how much I begged and pleaded, he refused to tell me anything about where she was.

Early the next morning I was tied up, gagged, and dragged from my cell before being led through the twisting stone corridors of the dungeons and up a flight of stairs. The guard dragged me by my wrist, and each time we turned a corner, he yanked me forward and I slammed straight into the wall. My body ached, and a scream built up inside me with each step we took. The nightmare scenarios that I'd imagined when Leon and I first came to Vilnaria—the fears of punishment or execution—were at last coming true.

The guard continued to drag me through the halls and out two large, wooden doors, into fresh air. I blinked as the sunlight overwhelmed my eyes. As my eyes adjusted, I spotted Kay and Ivan. They stood against the wall of the building I'd just exited. An imperial guard watched them with eyes sharper than the sword he was pointing at them. Two gallows lay in front of me, and a podium stood positioned between them, facing the city square. A large crowd of people gathered around the gallows, filling the air with a cacophony of voices. Eight imperial guards stood spread out around the edge of the crowd, holding their spears sideways—blocking the people from moving any closer.

I looked up at the building, and my eyes widened. The stone building with the bell tower loomed over me—the Court of Judgment.

The guard who had dragged me from my cell shoved me against the wall next to the others. Like me, the two of them were gagged. Ivan glared at me. His raven hair stuck out in all directions. He had a black eye and his arms were littered with scratches, cuts, and bruises. Kay stared straight ahead at the crowd. Instead of tied back, his long, dark hair hung limp, framing his face on both sides. And like Ivan, Kay's face, arms, and legs were covered in cuts and abrasions.

My gaze shifted to the left as Sir Fern exited the stone building, flanked by four imperial guards—two of which left the procession to join the guards in suppressing the crowd. Sir Fern wore a bloodred velvet uniform with black buttons and a heavy black cape. He walked forward, cane in hand and purpose in each step as he passed between the gallows and stood before the makeshift podium in front.

"People of Vilnaria, it is with a heavy heart that I begin today's execution ceremony," he began. "There is no joy in delivering justice. Only relief in knowing that the suffering of the innocent was not in vain." He glanced back at the three of us, his lip curled up far enough in disgust to brush his mustache. "These criminals are Myarnan spies and assassins. They *murdered* the Ivanyaran ambassadors that visited us in an attempt to sabotage good relations between Vilnaria and Ivanyar—good relations that our emperor has been striving to establish since the beginning of his reign."

4

My shoulders slouched as the crowd began yelling, calling for us all to be hanged. A man near the front of the crowd hurled something at us and I flinched as it hit the ground and splattered several yards away from us. A tomato.

Sir Fern raised his hands, and the crowd quieted. "During our investigation," he continued, "we found that these criminals are nothing but pawns, sent by the Myarnan leaders to undermine our emperor and destabilize Vilnaria by—"

"Make an example of them!" someone in the crowd shouted.

"Show 'em what happens when they mess with our emperor!" another person yelled.

Sir Fern spoke over the noise of the crowd. "Today, we'll see that justice is served!" He turned to the guards. "Bring the murderers forward."

The guards grabbed me and Ivan, dragging him toward the gallows on the left, and me toward the one on the right.

I twisted and squirmed, digging the heels of my boots into the uneven cobblestone, but the guard held on. He jerked me forward, throwing me off-balance.

I cried out as a sharp pain shot through my wrist, but the gag muffled the sound. The guard stepped up on the gallows's wooden platform, yanking me up after him. As he dragged me forward, my eyes landed on the thick loop of rope tied to the wooden beam towering over my head.

One more yank, and I was right in front of it. I could see the individual strands and fibers that had been twisted together to form the rope. My knees shook and my throat turned as dry as stale bread. My heart pounded within my chest, as if trying to break free of it. Death inched closer and closer with each second, but there was no way for me to run. Not this time. As the imperial guard grabbed the noose, the crowd grew louder, each shout and curse more vile and violent than the last. A sob welled up from inside me. As the guard slipped the noose over my head and around my neck, a woman screamed.

I looked up as more screams and shouts filled the air. The crowd parted and scattered to the sides of the square as mounted soldiers in pine-green uniforms rode into the square and through the crowd. There were at least fifteen, followed by a golden carriage bearing a shiny green insignia featuring a wolf. The carriage stopped, and a man with a familiar mane of blond hair emerged from within.

"Duke Gladik, what is the meaning of this?" Sir Fern yelled as the green uniformed soldiers surrounded the gallows and dismounted.

Duke Gladik glared at Sir Fern. "I believe I could ask the same of you, Sir Ferdinand! The people you are accusing of murder are innocent of that crime. And not only have you spurned their right to a trial, but you've denied them any opportunity to prove their innocence. This is a violation of our laws!"

Duke Gladik raised a hand, and three of his soldiers rushed forward. One of them headed straight toward me. The guard beside me took a step back, so I slipped my head out of the noose.

"Guards, take up arms!" Sir Fern yelled to the imperial guards. "Seize the duke's men and dispatch the prisoners—don't allow them to escape with their lives!"

His words brought life and energy surging back into my body. I half-hopped, half-stumbled toward the edge of the platform, but the imperial guard grabbed hold of my hair, wrenching me back. I let out a muffled cry, falling backward onto the platform. The guard reached for his sword, but as he unsheathed it, a soldier in green appeared.

"Head for the carriage!" he barked out, stepping between me and the attacking guard. I struggled to my feet as the soldier and guard clashed swords behind me.

All around me, the imperial guards and Duke Gladik's soldiers were fighting. I wriggled my feet back and forth, loosening the ropes that were binding my ankles enough to slip out of them. Now free, I dashed toward Duke Gladik and the golden coach, ignoring the clashing of steel and pained shouts and cries coming from all directions. I reached the duke, and Kay joined us seconds later.

"Get in the carriage," Duke Gladik said, turning to us.

"Duke Gladik," Sir Fern called. He stood straight and tall on the podium, his red hair neatly combed, and his mustache newly waxed. He held his cane out in front of him, and both of his hands rested on top of it. He stared directly at Duke Gladik. "I hope you realize that you're committing treason against Vilnaria *and* the emperor."

The duke whirled around, his teeth gritted and his blue eyes flashing with rage. "You're one to talk about treason, Sir Ferdinand, seeing as you're the one who holds the emperor's puppet strings." Duke Gladik looked to his men. By this time, they had managed to disarm nine of the twelve imperial guards, holding them at sword point. The other three imperial guards had retreated to join Sir Fern by the podium, swords and spears raised in defense.

"Arrest Sir Ferdinand!" the duke commanded the rest of his men, pointing at Sir Fern. The six remaining guards advanced toward Sir Fern and the podium, brandishing their own weapons.

Someone nudged my arm and I turned to see Kay, who nodded for me to get inside the carriage. I stumbled up the two steps. Ivan already sat inside on the green velvet-cushioned seats. I collapsed onto the seat across from him, turning my attention to my bound wrists.

Kay entered the carriage and sat next to Ivan. His large, muscular form took up his seat and part of Ivan's. Duke Gladik entered after, sitting next to me. The carriage rolled forward as the duke turned in my direction.

"Here, let me help you, Miss Amelia." He reached up and removed my gag. I let out a breath, moving my sore jaw around.

"Thanks," I mumbled.

Duke Gladik cleared his throat, glancing between the three of us. "I apologize for the delay in rescuing you. I would have been here a lot sooner, but I had several issues to deal with at my estate. If I had known that Sir Ferdinand of all people was behind the nobles' plot to conquer the north, I never would have let you go to the palace on your ow—"

"Where is Sadie?" Kay interrupted as he ripped his gag off, throwing it down by his feet.

My toes curled within my boots as my chest tightened. "I don't know…" I admitted.

Kay stared at me, his eyes piercing mine like daggers. "What do you mean you *don't know?* You were in the same cell, were you not?" His voice was strained, and his broad shoulders were stiffer than a statue.

I shrank beneath his gaze, staring down at my hands. They were scraped and smudged with who knew what. "Well, yes," I said. "We *were* in the same cell...but then guards came. They said she was wanted for questioning, took her away, and then..."

"And then what?"

I swallowed hard, clasping my hands tight enough to send pain through my fingers. "I...heard her screaming..."

Kay slammed his fist against the side of the carriage, and the entire vehicle shook as it rolled down the cobblestone street. He let out a string of curses, then ran a hand over his hair. "I have to go back," he said. "I *must* find her."

"I'll see if I can learn anything about her location," Duke Gladik said, "but I don't think it would be wise to return to the palace at this point in time."

I looked between both men. My chest ached, my arms trembled. "Do you...think she's...?" I stopped, unable to bring myself to finish that sentence.

Duke Gladik shook his head. "In all likelihood, she's still alive..."

Relief rushed through me. I sighed and closed my eyes, leaning back against the green-cushioned carriage seat. "Oh good...I was so worried when she—" I stopped and my eyes snapped open. I sat up, looking at the duke. "But wait, why would they take her from the cell in the first place?"

"So they can use her as a hostage," Kay spat. "Her father will be acting as Myarna's chief ambassador once he arrives, so he probably sees her as the perfect leverage."

I frowned. "He...you mean Sir Fern?"

"Who else?" Kay glowered in the direction of the carriage door. "He fully intends to do whatever it takes to start this war."

"Hold on!" Ivan held up a hand covered in bluish-purple bruises and minor cuts. His gag lay on his lap, stained with blood. His lips were chapped and swollen where they'd been busted. Between his dingy bloodstained shirt and his black eye, he looked less like a strong, capable mercenary, and more like a delinquent who started a bar fight he didn't win. "I'm going to need all of you to take a *big* step back and tell me what in thunderation is going on!" Ivan placed his hand on his chest. "I signed up for an *escort* mission, not to get arrested, beaten, and nearly executed for some kind of conspiracy that I had *nothing* to do with." His eyes shifted between the three of us. "What is even going on? Hostages? Traitors? War? And who was that walrus-faced crook with the stupid-looking mustache?"

I unclasped my hands only for them to curl into fists as anger burned within my stomach, growing stronger and stronger the more I thought about Sir Fern. "That man—the one who tried to have us executed—is Sir Ferdinand Richard Isaacs...the emperor's highest-ranking adviser," I said. "He's trying to frame Myarna for sabotaging relations between Vilnaria and Ivanyar so that Vilnaria will have a reason to go to war against us."

Ivan blinked. "And…how exactly did you and Leon get mixed up in all of this?"

I pressed my lips together and twisted some tangled strands of hair around my fingers. "Well…Leon and I made a mistake, and pretended to be ambassadors from Ivanyar—which ended up throwing off the Vilnarian nobles' plans to frame Myarna for the murder of the *real* Ivanyaran ambassadors who were traveling to Eldnaire a couple weeks ago."

Ivan stared at me. "You're crazy. You have to be… You're telling me Ivanyar is in on this too?"

The duke frowned at Ivan. "They aren't 'in on' anything. Emperor Kyvir decided that upon taking the throne he would establish peace throughout the entirety of the north."

"Peace? Yeah right," Ivan snorted. "If peace looks like invading, taking all the officials hostage and executing half of them before establishing their *own* ruling class, then sure…I bet he *does* want peace."

"No, it's true," I said. "I spoke with the emperor myself. I know that all he wants is peace. The empress dowager as well. We've had many discussions about their plans."

Ivan's jaw dropped. "You—*what?* You're joking."

I pressed my lips together and stared at my lap as I attempted to comb through my tangled hair with my fingers.

"Okay, so, you're not joking…" Ivan cursed like a sailor who stubbed his toe on a barrel of ale, then sighed. "All right, fine. Second question. Why didn't you tell me anything about this *before* dragging me into it?"

The carriage made a turn, and I leaned left to avoid bumping into Duke Gladik. I squirmed in my seat, then forced myself to look up at Ivan. "Well, you're…a mercenary… I wasn't sure I could trust you."

Ivan crossed his arms over his chest. "So you decided to *trick me* into walking straight into this blasted field full of cow patties?" He leaned forward, narrowing his eyes at me. "Wait—am I even gonna get paid for thi—"

"Enough," Kay interrupted. "The facts are, you're a part of this now. Whether you like it or not."

Ivan glared at Kay. "Absolutely not! The second this carriage stops I'm getting out and going home!"

Kay scoffed. "To Myarna? I hope you enjoy company because the Vilnarian army will be following in your footsteps. Face it… If something isn't done, we're *all* going to be in a lot of trouble."

"We're already in a lot of trouble," Ivan snapped. "We literally almost got executed just now!"

"But we escaped, and in the process we've learned that Sir Ferdinand is currently the one giving orders," Kay said, "which means that all the imperial guards in the city will be on the lookout for us."

"Sir Kay is correct," Duke Gladik said. "For now, the three of you need to stay out of sight. If Sir Ferdinand *is* in control, then I'm afraid that stopping war and rescuing Miss Sadie will be near impossible."

I looked out the window as we passed by taverns, shops, and inns, then lowered my hands to my lap as I let out a shaky breath. "I know that it might not be easy, but I…" I pursed my lips as an image of Sadie entered my mind. Her dark eyes and bright, mischievous smile. Then, another image flitted its way into my mind. One of Kyvir. Curly dark brown hair, a sweet smile, and warm hazel eyes. I clenched my fists. "I have to try," I said, my voice strengthened. "And if Sir Fern has harmed Sadie or the emperor in any way, I promise that I *won't* let him get away with it."

Two

We rode the rest of the way to the southeast end of the city in silence—though my mind was anything but quiet. Sadie was my best friend—someone who I knew I could always count on. But could she say the same for me? Could I really save her? And what about Kyvir? I wasn't politically savvy, I couldn't use a sword to save my life, and between Kay and Sir Fern, I was horrible at choosing the right people to trust.

Even so, changing the past was impossible, and the future was far too uncertain. I'd just have to focus on the present.

"Problems are only problems until they have solutions," the empress dowager—Marta's—words echoed in my mind. "Once they have solutions, they're nothing but challenges."

She had said that to me two days before I had left for Ivanyar with Leon, Kay, and Duke Gladik. The two of us were having tea in the garden when I decided to tell her my fears about the future—not just the looming threat of war in the north, but about my own, personal future.

"I think that this is a little more than a challenge, Marta," I said while frowning into my teacup. "I really like Kyvir, but as long as our countries are at odds…"

Marta smiled warmly, her hazel eyes filled with amusement. "Challenges may be difficult to overcome, but they *can* be overcome, dear. Just remember that you're not alone. There are plenty of people around you who are more than willing to assist you—myself included."

The warmth from Marta's smile melted away some of my worries, and I smiled back at her. "I know… I suppose I'm just feeling a little anxious. I went from having a clear future waiting for me at the library, to an uncertain one connected to the fates of three empires."

Marta shook her head. "No matter what happens, your future is *yours* to choose, Amelia. Whether you make the decision to return home to Myarna, marry my son, or anything else you wish to do." Once she finished speaking, the empress dowager paused, then studied me, her eyes sparkling with mischief. "Although, I think we both know what the best choice is out of those three things…"

She laughed as my face grew hot, then smiled at me once again. "But truly, Amelia. As much as I would love to see you and Kyvir together, your future is yours and yours alone. Don't get so wrapped up in the lives of others that you forget about your own. As a member of the royal family, I have always struggled to find a balance between duty and desire."

"So…how did you finally find it?" I asked.

Marta laughed. "Truthfully, I'm not sure I ever did. But

perhaps you can learn from my mistakes." She reached out and placed a hand on my shoulder. "Your family and country are important, but they aren't who you are."

I looked away at that, shifting my focus to a honeybee crawling across the table near my teacup. "I thought I was Amelia the librarian…but I don't know if that fits me anymore."

"Does it have to?"

I blinked at Marta. "I don't know… I guess not."

Marta hummed. "Well, perhaps you'll figure things out during your journey. Who knows? Perhaps we won't even recognize you when you return!"

The two of us had laughed. But that was before I had learned the truth behind the growing tension between the three countries. As nice as it was to imagine what living my own life would look like, I no longer had the right to think about it—at least, not until I had managed to find a way to stop Myarna and Vilnaria from going to war against each other.

I stared out the carriage window. The view had changed from townhouses, taverns, and the occasional inn to high-end dress shops, fancy restaurants, and small parks. The houses in this area were either freshly painted stone townhouses with well-manicured front lawns, or small cottages with thatched roofs and chickens or geese wandering around the yards.

When the carriage finally stopped, Duke Gladik helped me out and down. I looked up and stopped. "Are we…back at the palace?" I asked, only partially joking as I laid eyes on the large, luxurious building in front of me.

"Oh, right. This is the Von Gladik Manor," Duke Gladik explained. "I thought this would be the safest place for all of you to stay at the present moment."

My eyes drifted over the building again. Located in a quieter, wealthier part of the city, the duke's manor was only around half the size of the imperial palace, and the windows weren't as big, or as numerous. But between the brilliant green ivy growing up the sides, and the imposing stone wall encircling the manor and its grounds, it was almost just as grand. I turned to stare at the duke. "This is truly...*your* estate?"

He gave a small nod. "Yes, it's my family home."

"Huh." Ivan looked the manor up and down. "It really does look like another palace. Looks kinda old too... I'm surprised it wasn't torn down when Eldnaire was invaded."

"My father was Eldnarian and my mother was Vilnarian. They married shortly before the conflict," Duke Gladik explained. "Because of that, this estate remained untouched during Vilnaria's siege on the city."

"Must have been nice," Ivan said.

The duke frowned at him. "War is *never* nice."

Ivan waved his hand as if dismissing the duke's words. "Yeah, yeah... Now tell me how I can get out of this city without being spotted by the imperial guards."

"Are you sure you really want to try?" Kay asked. "Chances are you'll get caught. And then they'll want information."

"And I've got half a mind to give it to them," Ivan shot back. "In fact, I might not even charge them for it."

Kay narrowed his eyes. "As I'm sure you've noticed, Sir

Fern has a strict no-witnesses policy at the moment. Whether you talk or not, you *will* be silenced."

Ivan groaned. "Of all the—this is *not* what I signed up for! First, you take advantage of the bond between a teacher and his irresponsible protégé to con him into some *insane* conspiracy, and then you deny him his rights as a mercenary? At this point you're just being cruel."

Duke Gladik rubbed his forehead, letting out a deep sigh. "I will ensure that you are properly compensated for the time you spend here, Mr. Ivan."

Ivan eyed the duke. "You will?"

"Indeed." The duke placed his hand over his heart. "You have my word that you will be fully rewarded for your trouble."

Ivan's shoulders straightened, and a wide smile spread across his face. He clasped his hands together. "All right, so… how are we stopping this war?"

I shook my head and crossed my arms over my chest. "That was fast…" I muttered, eyeing him.

Ivan shrugged. "There's gold involved. I'm more than willing to listen now."

"Perhaps *you* are, but I have a responsibility to inform the rest of my subordinates about what's just taken place and allow them to make their choice." Duke Gladik frowned. "I… cannot be certain that many of them will wish to remain loyal to me after that."

"But didn't your guards swear on their lives to be loyal to your family?" I asked. "Doesn't that mean that betraying you would result in death?"

Duke Gladik nodded. "In most cases, yes. But since I've gone against the supposed wishes of the emperor, I've technically committed treason, and therefore have broken my right to loyalty…which means that my subordinates are free to defect or leave without any consequences if they so choose."

I frowned, watching the duke as he gazed toward his estate, a hand placed over his heart. He let out a deep breath. "But if any of them *do* decide to stay, I'll certainly be grateful. At the moment, I'm already aware of a few subordinates who will choose to stay and stand by my side." He dropped his hand from his chest and sighed. "The question is… How many of the others will choose to do the same?"

Nearly an hour later, Duke Gladik had what looked like a small army gathered in front of the Von Gladik Manor. There were easily a hundred people—if not more. Besides soldiers and guards, servants, cooks, and everyone else on his staff stood in the crowd.

Out of all of them, I only recognized one man—a tall man with a thin frame, short fair hair, brown eyes, and freckles scattered all over his nose and cheeks. He was the one who had called the duke back to his estate after our carriage had dropped us off at Eldnaire's city square—Francis.

A hum of whispers, murmurs, and quiet conversations emanated from the large crowd, but they all ceased the moment Duke Gladik spoke.

"I have just been labeled a traitor by Sir Ferdinand Richard Isaacs, and I have no doubt that other noblemen will reinforce his claim," the duke began. "I must, however, stay true to my convictions and continue my current course of action. I wish to get to the bottom of the crisis Vilnaria is currently facing—and if that makes me an enemy to Sir Ferdinand and the rest of the nobles, then so be it." He looked around at the crowd. "But this is *my* fight, not yours... And I won't ask you to take my side in this matter. If you wish to leave, you may do so now, and with my blessing."

"Duke Gladik, to call you a traitor is like calling a cat a horse," one of the men near the front of the crowd spoke up as he stepped forward, saluting the duke. "Many of us have had the honor of standing beside your father in the past, and now we choose to stand beside *you*."

Murmurs of agreement rippled throughout the crowd.

Duke Gladik's stiff shoulders relaxed. A smile spread across his face as he looked around. "And...is that how *all* of you feel?"

The crowd cheered, and Duke Gladik's smile widened. He glanced back at us, then turned to his men, nodding. "Very well... Then it appears we have work to do."

The next few hours were a whirlwind of introductions, instructions, and orders. The majority of Duke Gladik's subordinates decided to stay, and everyone worked together to secure and fortify the estate against spies, assassins, or any other attacks. Before long, rooms were prepared for Kay, Ivan, and myself.

Duke Gladik set a plan for us to meet later to discuss our next steps. And after he assured me that there was nothing more for me to do, I entered my guest room and collapsed onto the bed, allowing the haze of sleep to quickly overtake me.

After dinner, the duke called me, Kay, Ivan, and Francis into his main parlor.

Duke Gladik's main parlor was smaller than the one at the imperial palace, but what it lacked in size, it made up for in opulence. It boasted a white plaster ceiling with three small golden chandeliers hanging from it. The wallpaper was the same pine-green color as the Von Gladik insignia, with shiny golden swirls and floral designs. White upholstered sofas and carved walnut chairs created a crooked semicircle to face the grand piano that sat at the back of the room.

"There's no possible way that all of those people are really on your side," Ivan said. He lounged on one of the sofas to one side of the semicircle, while I sat next to Duke Gladik on another sofa across the way. Francis, Duke Gladik's aide, sat on the piano bench, and Kay sat on a wooden chair next to Ivan's sofa.

"You know what? I bet most of them just can't afford to quit," Ivan added.

"Whatever their reasons may be for staying, I'm still grateful that they chose to stay," Duke Gladik said with a sharp edge in his voice. "We'll need all the help that we can get."

"Stabbing someone while their back is turned isn't generally considered helpful," Ivan scoffed. "And blindly trusting people who *claim* to want to help you often ends badly—as I'm sure you've already discovered," he glanced between me, Kay, and the duke.

The duke glared at Ivan. "Many of these people and their families have served the Von Gladik family for *generations*. Would you have me interrogate them all as if they're nothing but criminals and traitors?"

Ivan shrugged. "Of course not. But keeping an eye on them would definitely be a good idea."

"Very well." Duke Gladik narrowed his eyes and lifted his chin. "Then that can be *your* responsibility."

Ivan frowned, sitting up. "I still haven't been paid for my *last* job, and now you want me to take on another one?"

"You are more than welcome to return to Myarna if that is where you'd like to wait for the Vilnarian army," the duke returned. "Although, I'm afraid I can't guarantee that you would make it there safely."

Ivan sighed, shaking his head. "You all better make this worth my while…"

"I will," the duke said. "I told you. You have my word."

"Yeah, yeah…whatever that's worth…" Ivan grumbled.

Duke Gladik squared his shoulders. "Mr. Ivan, I am a *Von Gladik*, not a mercenary. I *will* keep my word." The sharp edge returned to the duke's voice, and his blue eyes clouded with anger.

I played with the fabric of my skirt. "So what do we do now?" My voice wavered as I spoke. "Our plan was to talk to the emperor. But if Sir Fern has harmed him, or something else has happened, what can we do?"

Ivan sat up straight in his seat, choking on air. "Your plan was to...*talk*?" he spluttered. "That's not a plan... That's delusion meeting naivety for teatime in the land of dreams!"

"My first matter of business is to collect information," Duke Gladik said, ignoring Ivan. "Once I know the current situation in the imperial palace we'll be able to come up with a new plan."

I nodded. "That makes sense..."

The duke smiled, but it didn't quite reach his eyes. "If you need anything, just ask Francis or one of the servants. And until I can figure out what's going on, please... Make yourselves at home."

Ivan settled back onto the sofa with a wide smirk. "Oh, I *will*."

I sighed. More waiting. More wondering. And no answers. If what Kay said was true, then Sadie was imprisoned—which at least meant that she was alive. But how long would that be the case? And what about Kyvir? I never even had a chance to see him. Was he okay? And what would happen if he wasn't?

Three

Screams jolted me awake. In my mind, as I crossed the barrier from dreaming to wakefulness, I saw the girl in the forest—the Ivanyaran ambassador screaming in pain and fear. But this time, the girl's face belonged to Sadie.

I heard something crash in the hall outside my room and I kicked my covers back as I remembered where I was—Duke Gladik's estate.

I jumped from the bed and rushed to the door of my guest room. I threw the door open and stepped out into the corridor as hurried footsteps sounded from the right. I turned and froze in place. A figure wearing all black barreled toward me. His face was covered by a mask, and in his right hand he held something that glinted beneath the hallway's crystal lights. A dagger.

Fear stabbed at my beating heart, my feet frozen in place. As he came closer, I could see spots on the blade. Red spots. Blood.

He was only a couple yards away now. I forced myself to move, but it was too late. The man reached out—shoving me out of his way.

I yelped as I flew backward, falling to the floor just inside my doorway. Pain radiated through my back and the rest of my body. As I dragged myself to an upright position, three guards ran past my doorway after the figure. Right after them, Ivan appeared, but he stopped in his tracks upon seeing me on the floor. He wore a simple cream-colored nightshirt. His raven hair stuck out in all directions, and he wore mismatched socks—one gray and one black. But despite his disheveled appearance, his gaze was sharp and focused. "Oh, hey… You didn't get stabbed, did you?"

I stared up at him in a daze. "No, I…no…I'm fine."

I moved my legs and winced. Maybe fine was an overstatement.

Ivan stepped forward and offered me a hand. I gratefully accepted it, getting to my feet with his assistance.

"That was an assassin…" I said. My hands began to shake, so I clenched them. "There was blood on his dagger…" As I spoke, Kay joined us. Unlike Ivan and myself, he was fully clothed, even wearing his boots. His long, dark hair was tied back, and not a strand looked out of place.

Ivan frowned in the direction that the assassin had fled, then looked at me. "Well, he didn't attack you, and he didn't attack me, or him," he nodded at Kay. "So that only leaves—"

"Duke Gladik!" I gasped. I looked down the hall where the assassin had come from. My feet carried me in that direction, past the portraits and landscapes on the walls. Kay and Ivan followed. As I walked, Duke Gladik himself rounded the corner, followed by Francis and a couple guards. The duke wore a white nightshirt—stained with blood. He held a hand to his side, where the red was concentrated the most. Panic exploded in my mind as I rushed forward. "Duke! Are you all right?"

Duke Gladik's face was pale, but he managed a grimace. "It just grazed me," he assured me. He turned, dismissing the guards.

"The assassin—he ran right past me," I said as Kay and Ivan joined us.

"Don't worry, Miss Amelia, he won't get very far," Francis said, his voice low.

The duke nodded. "I have full confidence in my staff. They won't let the assassin make it off the grounds."

I let out a shaky breath, taking a step back as my head began to spin, filled with images of mercenaries and assassins in dark cloaks—like the ones who had nearly killed Leon. "That…that's good…" I began, "but why were you his only target? I thought he would have been after us…"

Kay opened his mouth, but Ivan interjected. "Actually, it makes complete sense. The duke is the only thing standing between us and that Sir Bern guy."

I blinked. "You mean, Sir Fern?"

Ivan scowled. "Yeah, whatever that lunatic's name is…" he grumbled. "All I know is that he wants us dead and buried."

I shivered, hugging my arms to my chest. "I don't understand... Why would Sir Fern bother sending assassins at all? Doesn't he have the imperial guards at his command? Why doesn't he make them come down and arrest the duke?"

"I can think of two reasons for that," Duke Gladik said, exchanging a glance with Francis. "Either he's afraid of stirring up anger among the people, or the emperor isn't quite as powerless as we originally believed."

"What?"

The duke winced, then sighed. "Now...is not the time to discuss this. It's late and we could all use some more rest. We'll meet and discuss this tomorrow afternoon once I have more information."

I frowned but nodded. "What if there are more assassins?"

"I've doubled the guard—inside the estate, and out. We'll all be safe until morning comes."

"Until morning comes?"

The duke gave me a thin smile. "I mean that there's nothing to fear, Miss Amelia... You may sleep peacefully."

I played with the ends of my long, dark hair. "I'm not certain I'll be able to sleep ever again..."

I eventually did fall back asleep, waking up late the next morning. Duke Gladik and Francis were busy dealing with matters of state, and Kay was nowhere to be found, so only Ivan joined me for breakfast, sitting down at the head of the table.

The dining room was fairly small compared to some of the other rooms I had seen in the duke's manor. The three large windows at the back of the dining room allowed the morning sunlight to filter into the room.

Instead of a huge table fit for feasts and banquets, a smaller oak table stood in the middle of the room. With three chairs on each side—one at the head, and one at the foot of the table—it looked more like the table my family used at home.

"Where is Kay?" I asked as I pulled a chair out from the table.

Ivan shrugged, his fork already embedded in his food. "Dunno. He was already leaving as I walked in here. He said something about taking a walk."

I pressed my lips together, staring at the plate of bacon, fruit, and bread in front of me as the strong scent of the bacon invaded my nose.

When Kay heard that Sadie was still back at the palace, he had wanted to go back immediately. Duke Gladik had convinced him to wait, and Kay hadn't brought it up since. What if that meant that he was planning to go rescue her without any help? And what if something went wrong? What could we do then?

"Huh. I'm beginning to think that your face was just made that way," Ivan said, studying me.

I blinked at him. "What?"

"Every time I look, it's all scrunched up with worry…like the face of a single mother of ten irresponsible boys who have no sense of self-preservation and a penchant for mischief."

I eyed him. "That's oddly specific…"

Ivan shrugged. "I'm describing my mother." He shoved a piece of bacon into his mouth.

My jaw dropped. "Wait," I stared at him. "You really have *nine* brothers?"

He swallowed, then grimaced. "*Had*. There are only six of us now…so I guess my mother had good reason to be worried."

"Oh…"

Ivan frowned. "Hey, don't look at me like that. I was trying to get you to stop worrying, but now you look like I just threw a rock at your dog."

"I don't have a dog…"

He raised an eyebrow. "Then why are you so upset?"

I couldn't help but smile. "You really do remind me of Leon…" I glanced toward the windows, catching sight of a blue sky, spotted with clouds. Speaking of Leon, he was probably fed up with resting in bed by this point. Perhaps he had already snuck out of the house a few times since I had left for Eldnaire along with Sadie, Kay, Ivan, and Duke Gladik. If he had, then our mother was probably at her wit's end with him.

Ivan smirked. "Like I said…I taught him everything he knows."

A breathy laugh escaped my lips. I didn't doubt it. Ivan's mother had probably had just as much trouble with him as my mother had with Leon—if not, more. "You're in a far better mood today," I noted as I picked up my fork.

Ivan's face lit up. "Of course I am. I took a…well, a *self-guided* tour of the manor earlier and saw the treasury."

I narrowed my eyes and pointed my fork at him. "You didn't steal anything, did you?"

He scoffed and waved his hand as if shooing away my words. "I'm a mercenary, not a thief…" Ivan leaned back in his chair and lifted his chin. "I only steal if someone *pays* me to steal. Besides, the duke was there… After his guards caught me snooping around," he added.

"Of course they did, it's their job." My gaze drifted back to the table. There was a white and green porcelain tea service sitting on a silver tray between me and Ivan, with four matching teacups laying face down on their saucers. Next to it was a pitcher of water. I reached out and grabbed the pitcher, pouring water into my empty glass.

Ivan flapped a hand at me. "Yeah, yeah… Anyway, now I have a little more faith in the duke's promise to pay me. He even gave me a really nice new sword as a down payment to make up for all the weapons the palace guard confiscated from me, so I'm actually in a *great* mood. I might just have to try the sword out later…"

My heart jumped within my chest. There it was. The perfect opportunity handed to me on a silver platter. I just needed to open my mouth and ask the question. I opened my mouth, but nothing came out.

Ivan eyed me. "Are you all right there? You look like a bass dying on a riverbank."

I put the pitcher down and swallowed hard, forcing myself to speak. "Um, yeah, I'm fine… I was just thinking… If you're going to be practicing with your sword, do you think that maybe…you could teach *me* while you're at it?"

Ivan stared at me. "Come again?"

I let out a deep breath, then spoke with a confidence I didn't feel. "I asked…if you would teach me how to sword fight…"

Ivan jabbed a thumb at his chest. "You want *me* to teach *you?*" He leaned back in his chair. "Are my ears hearing correctly, or have I finally gone daft in the head?"

My cheeks heated up. "It's not a big deal…I only want to learn how to defend myself…just in case. And you taught my brother, so perhaps…"

The corners of Ivan's mouth slowly twisted up into a smirk. "Perhaps I could use my advanced talents as a top-tier mercenary to instruct you in the art of swordplay?"

I looked away. "Something like that…" I muttered.

"Well, it's not like I have anything better to do. And it'll probably be pretty amusing to watch you struggle—I mean, learn."

I glared at him. "On second thought, maybe I don't want your help after all…"

Ivan clicked his tongue. "Oh, don't be like that. Rule one of sword fighting is *never* let your opponent get under your skin."

I frowned. "You're not my opponent, and we're not even on the training grounds."

Ivan held up two fingers. "Rule number two of sword fighting is that *everywhere* you go is a potential training or battleground." He added another finger. "And rule three is that *everyone* is your opponent. So don't let *anyone* get under your skin."

My frown deepened. "You're just making these rules up…"

Ivan smiled and shrugged. "Hey, they're good rules—words even—to live by. Here, what if I were to brandish my butter knife against you at this very moment? How would you respond?"

"Well, I…" I glanced around the table. "I suppose I'd throw the water pitcher at your head."

"And if I ducked?"

"My water glass."

Ivan's brow furrowed. "And what if I dodged that as well? Would you keep throwing things until you ran out?"

"Yes?"

Ivan shook his head and sighed. "I can see that I have my work cut out for me…"

"Why?" I narrowed my eyes at him. "What's wrong with my answers?"

Ivan crossed his arms over his chest. "Your weapon is always more valuable *in* your hand than out of it."

I tilted my head to the side. "Well, what about arrows?"

Ivan stared at me, then nodded. "Except for arrows."

"And crossbow bolts?"

"Same idea as arrows, so they're also an exception," he admitted.

"Well, what about throwing knives? They're specifically made for throwing."

"Except for those too."

"And what about—"

"Okay," Ivan interrupted, holding up a hand. "I think

that's enough questions for now. Let's finish our breakfast and head for the training grounds."

I raised an eyebrow. "Didn't you just say that *anywhere* was a potential training ground?"

"You learn quick…" Ivan narrowed his eyes at me. "Maybe a little *too* quick for my liking."

I gave him a tight smile. "I suppose that's just a Huld family trait."

Ivan shook his head. "Figures."

Four

From all his boasting and blustering I expected Ivan to be some sort of tyrant with a sword—barking out commands too fast for me to follow, forcing me to memorize a ton of odd terms and techniques, or immediately forcing me to spar with him.

As soon as we were at the training grounds, Ivan brought me over to the sword racks and unsheathed his own sword, handing it to me.

"Here's a sword," he said as I struggled to get a good grasp on it. "How does it feel? Can you imagine yourself swinging it?"

I looked at the sword in my hands. The blade glinted, the edge looked razor sharp. "I—"

"Be honest," he interrupted.

I glanced down at the sword again, then took a deep breath. "I suppose I can…"

Ivan grinned. "Great! Now, give it back."

"What?"

Ivan reached out, motioning for me to give him the sword. "Did you really think I was going to train you with a real sword during your first lesson?"

"Yes…?" I handed the sword back to Ivan.

Ivan sighed as he took his sword and sheathed it again. "Why do I even bother… Look, you need to get the basics down before I can have you swinging anything pointy around." He walked past me, over to the rack of swords. "I thought I was gonna have to train you with sticks at first, but luckily for us, the duke has actual training swords. Being rich must be pretty nice."

I watched him as he took one off the rack and examined it. Unlike Ivan's sword, these were scratched and lusterless. "They look really blunt…"

Ivan flashed a wide smile at me. "Exactly. That's what we want." He held the scuffed and scratched sword up in the air. "This'll give you a taste of what it'll be like to fight with a sharp sword—as far as weight and techniques go—but without the risk of you or me losing a limb."

"I'm not sure whether to be more relieved by your thoughtfulness or offended by the fact that you think I'm likely to harm us."

Ivan placed a hand over his heart. "Aww, you think I'm thoughtful?"

"Let's just start the training..."

Ivan shrugged. "As you wish."

35

The duke's training grounds were located to the left of the estate's gardens, blocked off by tall hedges. Half of the training grounds were dedicated to melee weapons like spears and swords, while the other half was set up to practice with ranged weapons like bows, throwing knives, and crossbows.

Since my goal was to learn swordsmanship, I stayed on the melee weapon side. A large wooden pole had been set up by the edge of the melee training grounds to practice swinging at, but Ivan stopped me before I could even take two steps toward it.

Instead, he had me stand in the middle of the training area, and for the first half of our training session, all he had me do was swing the sword—over and over again. He only ever stopped me to correct my posture, or have me reposition my feet. The repetitive movements were boring and monotonous, and it didn't take long for my arms to grow tired, but the slow pace of the training did erase a lot of the fear and dread that had been stewing around inside my stomach.

The drills and strict guidelines for posture and footwork made it feel more like piano lessons or studying for a test than preparing to possibly take someone's life.

According to Ivan, it was important that I developed good habits in the small things—form, technique, and position—before I moved on to anything else.

In fact, everything Ivan said was strangely…reasonable. He acted less like Ivan Lidare—the mercenary known for being as insufferable as he was skilled, and more like a real teacher. Patient, with a genuine interest in helping his students.

After going through several rounds of drills, I stopped for a much-needed water break while Ivan remained on the training ground. He held my training sword in his hand, and it was clear that he knew what he was doing. His gaze became sharp and focused the moment he took the blade. He fought against an invisible enemy—each thrust was calculated, and every parry had a purpose. His movements were quick and precise…unlike mine.

It was odd holding the sword in my hand, seeing the dull metal blade reflect sunlight as I practiced swinging it. It didn't feel right—and not just because my movements were clumsy and slow. Training and sword fighting still didn't feel like something Amelia Huld, the daughter of a librarian, should be engaged in.

But Amelia the librarian was gone now, and Amelia the traitor and former false ambassador needed to learn how to protect not only herself, but those that she cared for. So if that meant raising a blade, training hard, and putting all my effort into learning the proper techniques and forms, I would do it. And I would do it without any complaints.

Well, for the most part…

"Ivan…?" I said as I swung my sword—nearly missing the pole entirely.

"If you don't keep your eyes on the target then your swing goes off," Ivan said.

I lowered the sword, wincing as my arms ached. "Yeah, I noticed. Can we…stop now?"

Ivan blinked. "You're tired already?"

"*Already?* Haven't we been training for hours?"

He looked up at the sun, which was nearly directly overhead now. "Ah, I suppose we have… All right. Let's stop for now. We can pick back up later."

I rubbed my aching arms. "How about tomorrow after breakfast?" I suggested.

Ivan smirked. "What, you don't want to train all day?"

I glared at him. "My arms, legs, and back ache like I got trampled by a horse, and I'm pretty sure I pulled a few muscles that I didn't even know existed."

"It'll take a while, but it'll stop being so painful after you've had more training." He patted my shoulder. "Get some rest. You did good today."

My eyebrows raised at the compliment. "Thank you—"

"For a novice, of course," he amended. "If you were training to be a soldier you probably would have been thrown out of the army before you ever saw the first battle."

I sighed. "I should have known that your compliment would have a catch..."

Ivan grinned. "Nothing in life comes without a catch— even compliments." He held up four fingers. "That's rule number four."

"I still think you're just making these up..."

After lunch, I sat in the center of the duke's garden, staring into a large fountain. The water's gentle splashing sounds calmed some of my nerves, but my shoulders remained tense and sore from my training with Ivan.

Now that I had some time to myself, the reality of the current situation settled in. The Vilnarian citizens—apart from Duke Gladik's guards and staff, all believed me to be a murderer and a fraud.

They weren't completely wrong. I was certainly a fraud. But the title of *murderer* didn't belong anywhere near my name. It deserved to go straight to Sir Fern.

Somehow, things had gotten far more muddled and confusing than ever before, and questions swirled around in my mind—questions that I had no answers to. As much as I wanted to believe Kay and the duke's assumption that Sadie was alive and they were holding her hostage, it was still just that— an assumption. When I least expected it, her screams echoed through my mind and made my skin crawl.

I clenched my teeth till my jaw hurt, then my mind drifted from Sadie to Kyvir. Why hadn't he come to rescue us? What had Sir Fern done to him?

I had planned to stay in Myarna for fear of making things even worse than they were before, but the Council of Law hadn't given me that option. And if I gave up now, my family would be in danger. Either the council would deal with them, or the war would.

"Miss Amelia?"

I turned to see the duke approaching. His face was pale, and he had dark circles around his eyes. He held a hand over his wounded side.

I straightened my back. "Oh, Duke Gladik! How are you feeling? Do you have any news?"

The duke stopped in front of my bench. "The physician said my wound looks much worse than it really is, so as long as I take it easy for a little while I'll be just fine. And yes, I was actually just looking for you and the others—do you know where they are?"

"I know that Ivan is taking a nap in his room, but I have no idea where Kay is…"

The duke hummed. "I see. Well, I'll have a servant find them both so we can discuss what I've learned…but first, would you mind if I sat down?"

"Please, go ahead." I scooted over on the bench, making space for the duke.

The duke sat down beside me. "Thank you. I think it would be helpful for me to take a moment to clear my head," he let out a deep breath and rolled his shoulders back. "So much has happened, and yesterday was…quite the day. Really, the last *several* days have been quite trying."

I sighed. "I'm sorry…"

"It isn't your doing." He eyed me. "At least, not *completely.*"

I looked away as my fingers played with my dark hair, combing through it over and over again. Duke Gladik didn't need to remind me how this mess had begun. I was perfectly aware. "I never meant for things to get so far out of hand," I whispered.

"I'm certain you didn't. But here we are…on the precipice of war. You and the others are wanted fugitives, I've been labeled as a traitor, and I have a *mercenary*—of all people—living under my roof…"

"I heard that you caught him in your treasury."

The duke's eyes flashed. "Indeed I did. He even had the nerve to tell me which gold coins he wanted—and insisted that I give him a sword as part of his compensation to make up for the weapons he lost upon his arrest."

I blinked. That was a little different from the story that *I* had heard, but it definitely made more sense. My thoughts turned to my training session with Ivan that morning. "Ivan is…rather odd," I told the duke. "I'm not quite sure I understand him yet. He's certainly arrogant, and has a huge sense of entitlement, but he's a friend of my brother's, more bark than bite… And he definitely knows what he's doing when it comes to the blade. I'm…still not sure if he can be trusted though."

"And that's the one thing you *can* trust," the duke scoffed. "Trust that a mercenary will *always* be *untrustworthy*."

I gave the duke a faint smile. "Right…" My smile faded. "Do you think the emperor is all right?"

The duke ran a hand through his thick, blond mane of hair. "Truthfully, Miss Amelia, I'm not certain. I was perhaps more shocked yesterday than I should have been to learn that Sir Ferdinand of all people was behind the nobles and their warmongering. He's always been known as extremely loyal to the emperor and Vilnaria. I'm not certain what could have changed…unless he's decided that he wants the emperor's crown for himself."

My eyes widened as I stared at the duke. "Do you think he does?"

The duke clenched his fists. "He must. What other reason could he possibly have for doing this?"

"I don't know...in the dungeon he said something about being willing to sacrifice everything for the sake of the empire."

Duke Gladik scoffed. "Even now he wants to claim that he's doing all of this for the people? I don't believe it... This is nothing but selfishness and a thirst for destruction."

"We're going to stop him though," I said. "We *can't* let him win."

"No, we cannot."

A bird chirped from its perch atop a nearby hedge, and another sang in answer. The sweet smell of the flowers filled the air. Butterflies and bees flew over and around the fountain, buzzing or fluttering from flower bed to flower bed along the garden paths.

Duke Gladik let out a deep breath, scooting forward to the edge of the bench. "Well, we'd best get started with that meeting. I'll have a servant knock on the door to the mercenary's room, and send Francis to look for Kay."

"Have you been looking for me?" a deep voice asked.

I turned to see Kay walking toward us.

I managed a smile. "Yes, actually... Duke Gladik was just saying that we needed to have another meeting to discuss what he's learned."

"Indeed." The duke stood, and I joined him.

"Ah, it seems I'm right on time then."

I nodded. "I was a little worried when I didn't see you at breakfast this morning. I thought that maybe you had gone back to the palace…"

"No need to worry…" Kay smiled. "I spent the entire morning at the training grounds. By the time I finished it was lunchtime, so I decided to take a walk through the gardens and explore. It's truly beautiful here, Duke Gladik."

The corners of the duke's mouth turned up. "Thank you… We have some talented gardeners here on the estate. Shall we head inside now?"

"Of course. I'll go inform Ivan and meet you in the parlor." Kay strode toward the manor, followed by the duke.

I stared after their retreating forms, frozen in place.

The training grounds were large, but not *nearly* large enough for multiple people to train there without seeing each other. Ivan and I had gone there straight after breakfast, and had stayed there until lunchtime—just as Kay claimed that *he* had done. And yet, we hadn't seen any sign of him while we were there. So what had he really been doing? And why did he feel the need to lie about it?

The duke stopped and looked over his shoulder. "Miss Amelia? Is everything all right?" he called.

I blinked. "Ah, yes… My apologies…I'm coming!" I lifted the hem of my skirt as I jogged to catch up with the duke, but unease swirled around inside my stomach like a storm brewing in the sky.

Kay was a spy for the Council of Law, which meant

that in all likelihood there were many things that he had to keep a secret. But if we really wanted to stop Sir Fern and rescue Sadie, we needed to work *together*. Kay had to know that…right?

Five

*H*alf an hour later, we filed into the parlor, and everyone settled into their previous seats—Ivan lounging on the sofa, Duke Gladik and I on the sofa across from him, Francis on the piano bench, and Kay on the wooden chair.

"This is the situation as far as I can tell..." Duke Gladik opened a folder and glanced down at a small stack of reports. "A few days ago—just a day after we left—the news came out that the Ivanyaran ambassadors were murdered on their way back to Ivanyar."

My brow furrowed. "On the way *back* to Ivanyar?"

"It appears that you, Sir Kay, and your brother, are still regarded as the real ambassadors to the public," the duke said as he looked over the documents in his hands. "The story goes that the three of you left and were murdered."

Ivan raised an eyebrow. "And they expect everyone to believe that after murdering those ambassadors you went waltzing back into the city to present yourselves to the imperial guards?"

"No, it seems the events were altered in the reports," Duke Gladik tapped the papers. "There's no mention of your return to Eldnaire. Instead, the public was told that the guards captured you after pursuing you into the woods."

I dug my nails into the sofa's white fabric. "What a blatant lie!"

The duke pressed his lips together, scanning the papers in his hands. "Indeed…and yet, it worked. Sir Ferdinand has gained control over many of the imperial guards. That is how he managed to cover up the truth and paint you and the others as enemies of Vilnaria."

Enemies of Vilnaria. The words rang in my ears like alarm bells. Memories of the day before flashed through my mind— the angry crowd cursing and yelling, the man throwing tomatoes, and the noose that had been meant for my neck. It was a stark contrast to the smiles and greetings I'd been given at the spring festival when I walked around with Kyvir. *Kyvir…*

I swallowed hard. "And…what about Ky—the emperor? What's happened to him?"

The duke turned back to his reports. "After news spread about the supposed death of the Ivanyaran ambassadors, it seems that the emperor locked himself away in his office, and is hardly seen outside of it."

My stomach tightened. "Locked himself away, or *was* locked away?"

"That much is difficult to determine…" The duke sighed. "But either way, very few people have seen him since."

"Well, that's not a very good sign," Ivan remarked. "The

46

guy who's supposed to be running an entire empire is nowhere to be seen?"

"What we need right now is evidence," Duke Gladik said. "I must be able to prove to the people, and to the nobles who remain loyal to the emperor, that Sir Ferdinand is operating without the emperor's permission. With their support, I can take *direct* action. Without it, I'll just be another traitor in everyone's eyes…"

"What if you are, though?" Ivan asked. "What if war really is what the emperor wants, and you're just standing in his way?"

I sat up straight. "It's not! I know that if Kyvir knew what Sir Fern was doing, then he'd do everything he could to stop it." I turned to Duke Gladik. "Perhaps…perhaps we should try to get a message to him. I could write a letter to tell him that I really am alive."

Ivan wrinkled his nose. "What good would that do if he's being held prisoner?"

"None at all," the duke replied. "But my operatives are still unsure of the situation. If we could hear from the emperor himself, we'll know far more."

My toes curled over within my boots. "Right… And it's the quickest way to put a stop to all of this," I said. "Finding evidence against Sir Fern might take time—which we don't have a lot of. Before we left, Emperor Kyvir told me that some of his noblemen were planning to send troops here to the capital under the pretext of training them…when in reality, they'll be here to pressure the other nobles into joining the war faction."

Duke Gladik frowned and leaned forward in his seat. "Do you know when the troops will arrive?"

"He said that the troops would arrive within two weeks... but that was around ten days ago."

"Then they could be here any day now." The duke sighed. "If we can't stop Sir Fern before the nobles' troops arrive in Eldnaire, I'm afraid that we won't be able to stop the war."

My shoulders stiffened. "Then we *must* make contact with Kyvir. I know that once he finds out the truth—that there is no reason for Vilnaria to fight against Myarna—he'll stop Sir Fern and the nobles from stirring up the people."

"Eh, maybe—" Ivan yawned, "—though I still don't think a little note is going to help much. That evidence stuff the duke was talking about will probably be more effective."

Duke Gladik straightened his small stack of reports and slipped them back into the folder before closing it. "Very well. We're agreed then. I'll continue looking for evidence against Sir Ferdinand, and in the meantime, we'll attempt to send a message to the emperor." He turned to Francis. "Francis, will you please go find Miss Amelia some parchment and ink?"

Francis stood and gave the duke a salute. "Of course, sir." The lanky man turned and wove his way through the furniture as he headed for the parlor door.

Once the door closed behind him, Ivan glanced between all of us. "All right, let's say you *do* get the message to the emperor. What if it turns out that he *is* fully in control of his decisions?"

"He can't be," I said. "At the very least, I'm certain that he's not aware of what's happening with Sir Fern or about the execution..."

Ivan stared at me. "You've got to be one of the most naive women alive... He's the *emperor*. How could he *not* be aware of what's going on inside his own palace?"

Before I could open my mouth, Kay spoke. "There's no use in speculating until we can gather more information. For now, we'll just have to wait and see if Miss Amelia's message will actually get through to the emperor." He glanced at Duke Gladik. "And, of course, as the duke said, evidence against Sir Fern will help."

"I hate waiting," Ivan grumbled. "But I suppose that as long as I must, I should enjoy the perks of living the noble life... These chances aren't easy to come by after all."

The duke sighed and stood. "You're welcome to do so. I simply ask that you remain respectful to my staff, and stay out of trouble."

Ivan grinned at the duke. "My middle name is respect."

The duke wrinkled his nose. "I highly doubt that."

"Okay, fine, you're right. I don't even have a middle name..." Ivan admitted, "but I'll have you know that I can be *very* respectful...for the right price."

Duke Gladik stood. Irritation flickered in his blue eyes. "I have work to do," he muttered before stalking toward the door.

As the door closed behind the duke, Ivan turned to me. "Hey Millie..."

"It's Amelia."

"What's rule one of sword fighting?"

I gave him a wary look. "Don't let your opponent get under your skin."

Ivan nodded, glancing at the door. "I don't think the duke ever learned that rule."

"Well, he didn't have *you* as an instructor."

Writing a letter to Kyvir proved far more difficult than I expected. How was I supposed to fit everything that I wanted to say within the confines of one small piece of paper? The important thing was letting him know that I was alive, but there was so much more I could say. Like how much I've missed our walks in the garden, or our deep, hushed conversations in the library—or our dances. Especially our dances.

Kyvir was no longer an emperor to me… He was a friend. Well, more than a friend. He was someone whom I liked—a lot. Actually, more than a lot. My face was growing hot just thinking about his warm hazel eyes and deep laugh.

And besides the content, there was the technical side of writing—the actual words. "Dear Kyvir" felt too formal, but "Dearest Kyvir" felt too lovestruck. And "Greetings from the Gladik estate where I'm currently staying in order to avoid getting murdered by your closest adviser" seemed inappropriate.

The desk in my guest room was covered in a snowfall of crumpled up papers but I still had nothing to show for it—and the letter needed to reach Kyvir as soon as possible.

I groaned and leaned back in my chair. Perhaps I was overthinking this. What I really needed to do was try *not* thinking. Maybe that would work better than agonizing over every single word.

I sat up straight and grabbed the pen, putting it to parchment once more.

Dearest Kyvir,

I'm not dead. Don't be deceived by those who tell you that I am. I am alive, well, and anxious to see you again. Please stay safe, and don't trust Sir Fern. He pretends to want peace, but is actually on the side of war.

My space is limited, so please, if you can, think of an excuse to leave the palace, and come see me at Duke Gladik's mansion. I'll explain everything to you.

Be careful, Kyvir. I'd never forgive myself if anything ever happened to you.

Eternally yours, Amelia

Eternally yours. I had written without thinking, and that was the result. I shook my head as if that would get rid of the deep blush I could feel taking over my entire face. I reached for the message, ready to crumple it up, but stopped short of touching the paper.

If that was how I really felt, then what was wrong with sending it?

Before I could change my mind, I picked up the note and folded it into a neat, tiny square, clutching it as if it would fly away at any moment if I didn't. I pushed my chair away from the desk and stood, turning and walking over to the door. I turned the knob and pulled it open only to come face to face with a set of knuckles. The knuckles stopped moving inches from my nose. I looked up to see a young man with a round face, reddish-brown hair sticking out from beneath a green cap, and wide blue eyes. "Oh, my apologies, miss." He dropped his fist and the corner of his mouth turned up into a smile. "I'm Tristan. I was just coming to ask about the note I'm supposed to deliver to the palace. Mr. Francis sent me."

I looked down at the note in my hand, then looked up at the messenger. "There's no need to apologize... I...I have the note right here." I reached up, offering him the folded paper.

The man took it and nodded. "I'll see to it that your message is delivered, miss. You have my word."

I managed a smile despite the knots in my stomach. "Thank you...and be safe."

The messenger tipped his hat to me, then turned and started down the hallway. I watched him go, but as he turned the corner, regret started gnawing at my mind. Did I say the right things in the letter? Was it a mistake to have used the word "dearest" in my address? Was "eternally yours" too extreme? What if he thought that the letter was forged?

The questions swirled around inside my mind until I couldn't take it anymore. My feet started moving down the hallway, after the messenger. I was right. A note couldn't say everything that I needed it to say. But *I* could. And there would be no denying that I was alive if I was right before Kyvir's eyes.

I slipped through the hall, past servants and guards. Some smiled and nodded, others ignored me completely. I turned a corner, but the messenger was nowhere in sight.

I kept walking, scanning the halls for any trace of Tristan as I went.

Finally, I spotted his green cap. He was walking toward the estate's west entrance—far ahead of me. I sped up, but Tristan was out the door long before I could catch up. Once I reached the end of the hallway, I opened the door and rushed out into the sunshine. The sky above was clear and blue, allowing the sun full access to everything below it. I squinted as my eyes adjusted to the sharp change in brightness. Tristan had already walked down the stone path and was waiting for a guard to open the side gate for him. I hurried down the path toward the gate, watching as Tristan exited the estate's grounds. The guard at the gate started to close it, but stopped upon seeing me jog near. I nodded and mumbled a thank you to the guard as I stepped through the gate, my pace slower than before.

What was I thinking? Going to the palace without a plan was a *terrible* idea. I'd be recognized right away, and then I'd end up back at the gallows. Maybe my letter didn't quite say everything that I wanted it to say—like how much I missed spending time with Kyvir, or that I had started learning swordsmanship—but as long as my note reached him safely, I'd have every opportunity to tell him everything.

I stopped walking around ten steps from the gate and started to turn around, only to spot Kay walking toward me with a deep frown on his face, his eyes trained on the ground.

I stepped toward him. "Kay?" I called.

His gaze snapped up to meet mine. "Miss Amelia? What are you doing out here?"

"I...I was seeing the messenger off..." I stammered, my cheeks burning. "What are you doing?"

Kay let out a laugh. "Me? Oh, I was just taking a little stroll... That's all. Shall we head back to the estate?"

I studied Kay's face, noting the dark circles under his eyes. "All right... You look like you could use some rest."

"I'm fine. I simply have quite a bit on my mind... That's all. Come, let's return before anyone grows worried."

Kay offered me his arm and I took it, allowing him to escort me back toward the manor. I looked closer at his face as we walked. He was pale and gaunt, and several strands of his long, dark hair had escaped from his hair tie. "You're worried about Sadie, aren't you... But didn't you say that she would be all right?"

"I did. And it's true. Sadie *will* return to Myarna unharmed." Kay's jaw clenched. "I'll make sure of it."

I pressed my lips together. Something told me that it wouldn't be quite as simple as Kay made it sound.

Six

*D*espite him being brash, arrogant, and bordering on narcissistic, I was lucky to have Ivan as a teacher. During our training the next morning after breakfast, it became even more clear that I was in good hands.

Before we began warming up, Ivan sat me down on a bench to discuss tactics—the best way for me to win against an attacker should I find myself in danger again.

"I usually tell my students to go for the head, but I doubt you'd even be able to reach the shoulders of most of your opponents, so stick to the lower half, and watch out for strikes from above," he said, looking me up and down. "Cause that's probably all you'll ever face."

I crossed my arms. "Can't you teach me *without* insulting me?"

"I could, but it wouldn't be nearly as helpful," he smirked. "Like I said before, the best way to win against your opponent is attacking their mind. Their body is just extra."

I shook my head. "Insults and mind games are not my area of expertise…"

"Yeah, I noticed. But we'll work on that. For now, let's focus on what you *can* do." Ivan pulled a small piece of paper out of his pocket and unfolded it. He glanced at me, then scanned the paper. "While you attack, your thoughts need to be focused on defense. Your opponent's size, speed, weapon length, experience, and even their expression should influence the way that you fight and defend yourself. Don't make your swings obvious—your opponent is gonna know exactly where you're going to hit before you even get to swing your sword forward. Because of your size, you're going to have to rely on your speed, agility, reflexes, and body reading."

I blinked. "That's…a lot."

Ivan chuckled. "Don't worry… I'll walk you through it all." He stood up, then offered me a hand. "Come on. Let's get you warmed up, then practice defense tactics for a bit."

I took his hand and stood. "All right… Let's do it."

"Oh, by the way, I was wondering…" he glanced at me. "What exactly is up with you and the emperor?"

I averted my gaze. "What sort of question is that?"

"The type that can make you turn redder than a rose in full bloom, apparently," Ivan snorted.

"It's not what you think…"

Ivan started the stretches, reaching an arm up and over his head. "You don't know what I think," he said.

"I'm pretty sure I could guess…" I retorted, copying the stretch, "but Kyvir and I only met a few weeks ago."

56

Ivan smirked. "So, he's *Kyvir* to you."

"It's not like that!"

Ivan switched arms. "You talk an awful lot about how things aren't, but I'm more interested in hearing about how they *are*. So…" he eyed me. "Are you and the emperor lovers?"

I choked on my own saliva and started coughing. Ivan patted me on the back until the coughs subsided, and I glared at him. "Why does everyone keep assuming that?"

"Probably because of your reaction," he said, smiling brightly.

I looked away. "We're not lovers… We're just…friends…"

"Just friends?"

"Well, for *now* we are," I admitted. "But the empress dowager—"

Ivan raised an eyebrow. "So you've met the former empress as well? What's she like?" he asked as he went back to stretching his arm.

I also continued stretching. "She's…different from what I was expecting. I always thought that the wife of the late emperor would be as cold, cruel, and vicious as he was… But Marta's like a warm ray of sunshine. Despite the fact that I'm nothing more than a librarian, she insists that I treat her casually and call her by her given name." I smiled. "And she definitely gives the best hugs…"

Ivan switched from arm stretches to lunges. "You befriended the emperor *and* his mother? You're really doing your best to marry above your station aren't you…"

"I would never dream of it! At least not if the empress

dowager hadn't suggested the idea…"

Ivan stared at me. "What…?"

"She said that even though I'm not of noble blood, my family is respectable enough that a marriage would be possible—and could even help stabilize relations between Myarna and Vilnaria," I winced as my leg muscles protested against the lunges.

"Interesting…"

I glanced at him. "What is it?"

He shook his head. "Nothing… I was just thinking." He eyed me. "Hey, don't go around telling people this stuff, all right?"

"The only reason I said anything was because you asked…"

"Then you're the type of person who could put an interrogator out of a job," he snorted. "Remind me never to tell you any of my secrets."

"I don't *want* to hear your secrets. I've had quite enough of secrets and pretenses... I just want to be done with them."

"In that case, you might wanna rethink the whole empress thing," Ivan said. He stopped stretching and straightened.

I also straightened. "What?"

"You really think your empress dowager managed to outlive her husband by being honest and straightforward?" Ivan rolled his shoulders back. "Everyone wears a mask of some kind. The only difference between nobles like them and commoners like us is that we can actually take the mask off now and then. The nobility can't afford to show any weaknesses. If they do, they won't last long. That's why we're currently in this mess, isn't it? Because the new emperor made the mistake of wearing a crown without a mask."

I frowned. "Being honest isn't a weakness."

"No, it's not... Not until you need to survive, that is." Ivan turned to face me and his brown eyes met mine. "Look, Millie... I may not be the oldest stone in the stream, but I've seen a lot in my thirty-five years of living, and trust me... Good endings usually have bad beginnings. If you don't play by the rules of the world, then the world will play *you*."

I looked away. Ivan was a mercenary. Of course he only saw the darkness in the world. Marta and Kyvir were different. They were warm and kind—honest and sincere. They weren't like Ivan.

"Anyway, enough of that," Ivan said, flashing me a grin. "I'd say you're good and ready for today's training. Let's begin." He turned and headed for the weapon racks while I watched.

My second day of training with Ivan was even harder than the first. My hands had started blistering from the constant rubbing and swinging, and by halfway through our training, my arms and legs ached even worse than they had the day before.

I could see the progress I had made though. My posture and movements weren't so stiff and rigid. My swings—though still a little weak and mistimed—were far more accurate than the day before. And thanks to the regular exercise, my strength and stamina had improved. Instead of needing a break every ten minutes, I could go for an entire twenty.

But even with all the improvements I'd made, I was still more than happy to stop once the servants came out to inform us that lunch was served in the dining room.

After lunch, Duke Gladik and Francis went back to the duke's office to work while Ivan went to his room to take his daily nap. I wandered about the halls like a restless phantom, feeling about as useful as a table with no legs.

It was just like my time in the palace. When Kyvir was busy with matters of state and Leon was busy talking up all the nobles, I was left with nothing to do but sit or walk in the gardens, read books in the library, worry, or explore.

It made me wish that I had something—anything to do. I'd gladly dust furniture, wash clothes, or sweep the floors if only to occupy myself with *something*. An added bonus would be the fact that I could repay the duke for his kindness.

Unfortunately, my plans of earning my keep didn't last long. The moment I asked the head maid where I could find a broom, I was lectured into oblivion. "Guests don't do housework," and "If I ever catch you with a dust rag there *will* be consequences!"

With that door closed, I continued wandering through the halls until I spotted two large, ornate wooden doors at the end of the hallway. I walked over and peeked inside the slightly open door. Tall shelves stood in neat rows, and the smell of old books wafted into the hall. A library.

I smothered a squeal. Finally, I had *something* to do. Perhaps I could research more about Vilnaria and the royal family—or even Sir Fern. My stomach tightened.

I pushed the door open farther and tentatively stepped inside. My feet padded across the carpeted floor. As I walked, I spotted a familiar figure sitting in a chair, engrossed in a book. "Kay?"

Kay's gaze shot up to meet mine as he slammed the book down on the table in front of him. "Oh… Miss Amelia." His shoulders relaxed. "It's you…"

I blinked. "Uh, yes…is everything all right?"

"Yes, everything is fine," Kay smiled. "My apologies, you simply startled me." He stood.

"I'm sorry…I didn't mean to disturb you…" I shook my head. "I wasn't expecting that anyone would be in here."

"It's quite all right." Kay cleared his throat. "I suppose you're coming here from lunch?"

I nodded. "That's right. Where have you been all morning?"

Kay pushed his seat in. "Ah, just at the training grounds."

He was lying. Again.

I crossed my arms. "Really? I didn't see you there."

Kay didn't so much as blink before he spoke. "Oh, I wasn't there long since I had some letters to write. What were you doing at the training grounds?"

"Training," I replied.

Kay raised an eyebrow. "Oh?"

"I thought it would be wise."

Kay nodded. "Fair enough. Perhaps I can assist you at some point."

I tilted my head to the side. "Really?"

"Of course." His lips turned up into a smile that didn't

reach his eyes. "It would be my pleasure. Now, if you'll excuse me...I need to go mail my letters." He started for the door.

"Kay, wait..."

He stopped, turning. "Yes, Miss Amelia?"

"You didn't really go to the training grounds yesterday," I said. "And you didn't go today either."

Kay rubbed his temple then let out a deep sigh. "Miss Amelia...the two of us have the same goal."

I narrowed my eyes at him. "Do we really?" I couldn't mask the suspicion in my voice. The sting of Kay's betrayal in Myarna still lingered at the back of my mind, slowly chipping away at what little trust I still had in him.

Kay stepped forward, his gaze meeting mine. "You want Sad—Miss Dourain to remain safe, do you not?"

I frowned. "Of course I do!"

"Then we indeed have the same goal."

"But if that's the case, then why won't you work with the rest of us? Or at least tell us your plans?"

"Because I have no desire to reveal my identity as a Myarnan spy to the duke," Kay said.

I pursed my lips. "Still...we could help you...the *duke* could help you."

"I have no need of his help." Kay gave a dismissive wave of his hand. "It would only complicate matters." He looked me in the eyes. "Miss Amelia, please trust me in this. I can ensure that Miss Dourain returns home safely."

"The last time I blindly trusted you, I found out that your

real name is Benjamin, and you turned me over to the Council of Law," I reminded him.

"I knew that under the circumstances, you would not be sentenced to death."

I frowned. "Still…"

"Miss Dourain does not deserve to die simply because she wished to be a good friend to you."

My eyes widened. Guilt pierced my heart like a dagger. I stepped back and nearly tripped over the table Kay had been sitting at. My hands shook, and the bitter taste of bile filled the back of my mouth. "You can't blame me for that!" I choked out. "I tried to dissuade her from coming—we all did!"

"My apologies…I didn't intend to make it appear as if I blamed you for Miss Dourain's decision," Kay lowered his voice. "What I'm *trying* to say, is that Miss Dourain's time is limited. If I don't act before her father arrives, then her life will be in far more danger than it is now. So please, Miss Amelia… Trust me with Miss Dourain's safety."

I stared at Kay. Sincerity shone in his eyes. It was obvious how much he cared for Sadie, and yet I couldn't help but feel slightly uneasy. But he was right. I swallowed hard, but nodded. "Very well…" I said quietly. "I trust you…"

Kay gave me a thin smile. "Thank you, Miss Amelia. You won't regret this." He turned and left the library.

I slowly shook my head. I clasped my shaking hands and brought them up to my chest. As much as I wanted to believe him, a voice deep inside of me whispered that I had just made a terrible mistake.

As I walked into the parlor that evening, something felt off. Ivan sat up on his sofa instead of lounging, Kay sat with his muscular arms crossed and his brow furrowed, Francis was looking through a folder of documents, and Duke Gladik paced back and forth within the semicircle of furniture, running a hand through his mane of blond hair.

I walked toward my seat, watching everyone. "What happened?"

Duke Gladik stopped pacing and looked at me. His blue eyes were filled with pain. "Tristan, the messenger Francis sent to deliver your letter… He's dead."

I stared at the duke. My brain couldn't seem to process his words. Tristan. Messenger. Dead. I found myself falling backward, collapsing onto the sofa.

The duke sighed. "I've been thinking. Perhaps I should try to speak with the emperor myself."

Francis shot to his feet. "Absolutely not!" The lanky man blinked, then cleared his throat. "Sir," he added before continuing, "if you attempt to leave the estate without adequate protection, you'll be in terrible danger. We cannot afford to lose you…"

"What he said," Ivan spoke up. "You are our shield after all."

I glared at Ivan. How could he say something like that after a man was just— "Is that really all you're worried about?" I snapped.

Ivan shrugged. "No, of course not. I want my money too."

"In any case," Kay glanced between me and Duke Gladik, "it appears that messaging the emperor is not an option at this point."

My stomach twisted. "Well... What about Marta—I mean, the empress dowager? If we can reach her, then perhaps she could help us. Maybe she could even get a message to the emperor."

"Indeed," Kay said. "I doubt there are nearly as many people watching the empress dowager's movements. Not compared to her son's."

Duke Gladik stepped over to the sofa and sat down next to me. "It's certainly worth a try..." He let out a deep breath. "All right, I'll have one of my operatives attempt to get a message to the empress dowager to arrange a meeting with her."

Ivan looked up. "Hey, speaking of which, how has your search for proof been going? Find anything yet?"

Duke Gladik frowned. He exchanged a glance with Francis before looking around at the rest of us. "Forgive me, but I'm still waiting on a few reports. I will inform you of any updates later."

I nodded. Proof of Sir Fern's wrongdoings would be helpful, of course, but a spark of hope lit within my heart at the thought of seeing the empress dowager again. I had no idea what Marta knew, or what she had heard. But if there *was* a chance that Marta would believe us—that she would help us—then we had to try.

Seven

*B*y my third day of training, the truth was becoming perfectly clear, and I finally had the courage to admit it.

While it was difficult, and every bone in my body always ached after I was finished, I really enjoyed working with the sword. There was something exhilarating about holding the sword in my hand and understanding how I was supposed to use it—like knowing a secret code.

Could I fight off an entire army of mercenaries? Or hold a sword for more than twenty minutes without my arms getting tired? No…but at least I was improving. Ivan started sparring with me toward the end of our third session—at probably a tenth of his usual speed and skill—but I'd say it counted.

It turned out that stance was one of the most important parts of fighting against an opponent. Too wide of a stance and I wouldn't have enough balance, or be able to react quickly to his attacks. Too narrow and I faced the same problem.

But as long as I bent my knees just right and paid attention, I could usually manage to see his attacks coming and act fast enough to adjust my stance and parry his strikes.

After the sparring match, I allowed myself to collapse onto the bench on the perimeter of the training grounds before grabbing my canteen and taking a large sip of water.

"Hey Millie, don't you think the duke was acting a little odd during yesterday's meeting?"

I glanced at Ivan. "What do you mean?"

Ivan's nose scrunched up, and he wore a frown. "He wasn't exactly jumping to give us any details about his investigation."

"Well, he did say that he would tell us as soon as he had any updates," I reminded him.

"No… He said that he would tell us about any updates *later*." Ivan sat down next to me. "Which means that he does have some updates, but he's not planning to tell us anything until he decides it's safe."

I frowned. "Safe? What do you mean? Why wouldn't it be safe to tell us?"

"If one of us was a spy it wouldn't be safe."

I blinked. "But we aren't spies…"

"You and I may not be spies, but I have a feeling that *someone* is leaking information." Ivan shook his head. "If the duke's messenger had any skill, he would have been able to blend in without drawing any suspicion. Which means that even if he wasn't able to get too close to the emperor, he probably wouldn't have been caught and killed—unless the people at the palace knew ahead of time to look out for him."

My eyes widened and my breath caught in my throat.

"You think Duke Gladik believes that one of us is responsible for Tristan's death?"

"There's no doubt in my mind. Only the five of us and the messenger himself knew about the note, and guards usually aren't the hardest rocks to fool. It's more believable that there's a traitor in our midst than that the imperial guards are actually competent."

My mind immediately jumped to Kay, but I shook my head. Kay had been serious about keeping Sadie safe. He wouldn't betray us—at least not in this particular situation. "Still...there's no proof that one of us is a traitor."

Ivan shrugged. "Maybe not yet, but just give me a couple days and I'll root 'em out. Just you wait, Millie."

I pressed my lips together as my fingers played with the lid on my canteen. "I hope you're wrong... I hope there isn't a traitor."

"Ah, come on, don't be all gloomy. If I am wrong, then maybe the duke's note will make it to your empress dowager friend."

"Right." I let out a deep breath. "If she gets the message without any problems then it would prove that none of us are traitors."

"Yeah, although even if she does get the message we still gotta hope that she likes you enough to actually do something about this situation."

I frowned at Ivan. "Of course she'll do something. Marta is a strong advocate for peace."

"Confidence," Ivan nodded. "I can appreciate that...as long as it doesn't get me killed, that is. I'm still a little bent by the fact that you didn't give me any details about this mess when you hired me."

"Like I said before, I didn't know if I could trust you." I stared down at my boots. They were covered in a thick layer of tan dust from the dry dirt of the training ground.

Ivan hummed. "Eh, fair enough, I suppose." He turned his gaze toward me. "But look…Myarna is my home, same as yours. I'm not about to let those Vilnarian brutes destroy it. Not without a fight."

Guilt ate away at my thoughts. I had been so focused on the fact that Ivan was a mercenary who only ever talked about money. I hadn't even considered the fact that Ivan might also have other reasons to stop the war. "Does your mother still live in Myarna?" I asked.

He nodded. "With my little brothers." A smile played at Ivan's lips. "The youngest one's probably around ten now."

I found myself smiling as well. "Oh… Does he also want to be a mercenary?"

"Better not!" Ivan scowled. "That boy is going to get a position on the Council of Law one day. He's not going to waste his life swinging around a sword and drinking watered down beer."

I tilted my head to the side. "You mean like you do?"

Ivan recoiled, staring at me as if I had just insulted his honor beyond repair. "Hey now…what I do isn't a waste." He puffed out his chest. "I'll have you know that I am a *respectable* mercenary who makes a *respectable* wage…when I'm not showing pity toward my former student's younger sister, that is..."

I placed my canteen down on the bench next to me. "And yet you want your brother as far away from your career as possible."

"He's a bright kid," Ivan said quietly. "With all the options available to him, why shouldn't he choose something else?" He suddenly flashed me a smile and stood. "Okay, I think we've rested long enough. Ready to get back to training?"

My body protested the idea, but I dragged myself to my feet. "Right…of course." I was wrong about Ivan. Like Leon, he did care, he just didn't want anyone else to know it.

Duke Gladik, Francis, and Kay were already at the table by the time Ivan and I walked into the dining room for lunch. All three men had furrowed brows and pinched lips.

"Did something happen?" I asked.

Duke Gladik stood. "Miss Amelia, please, join us."

"Hello to you too, Duke…" Ivan grumbled as we walked over to the table.

Duke Gladik pulled a chair out for me, and I sat down, nodding my thanks. I watched the duke as he returned to his seat. After sitting, he looked up at me. "This morning an ambassador from Myarna arrived."

I froze. An ambassador from Myarna? That could only mean… I straightened in my seat. "Mr. Dourain?" Hope infused my question.

The duke nodded. "Indeed. It caused quite the stir. Several young people followed his carriage through town, throwing rocks at the windows. One of them even cracked the glass."

"Huh. That never would have happened if it were a Vilnarian ambassador visiting Myarna," Ivan said as he sat down. "Not because they wouldn't *want* to throw rocks at the ambassador, but because they'd be too scared of the consequences."

The duke sighed. "Normally there would be harsh consequences for anyone who mistreated an ambassador in Vilnaria as well."

I stared down at my plate. "Then I suppose things truly are getting worse…"

"Indeed."

Ivan held up a hand. "Hold on…this Mr. Dourain ambassador guy…he's not *Dirk* Dourain, member of the Council of Law, and the Head Magistrate's assistant…is he?"

"Why do you ask?"

Ivan stared at me. "Why do I—how is it that you've managed to meet some of the most influential people in the north and yet you treat it like it's normal?"

"I've known Mr. Dourain for a long time. He and his wife are friends with my parents, and I…I'm friends with their daughter, Sadie."

"Wait, that was the girl that was traveling with you— she was—" Ivan shook his head. "Yeah, this is definitely the weirdest job I've ever taken…"

I cleared my throat as if that would also clear away my worries, then looked up. "I think we should talk to Mr. Dourain. I'm sure he would know what we should do about all of this."

"Absolutely not," Kay said, placing his fork down on his plate, "Giving Mr. Dourain any information would not only put *him* in danger, but Sadie as well."

I frowned. "But isn't he already in danger?"

"His status as an ambassador will be enough to shield him from any major harm," Kay replied. "Even in the event of a war. He's worth more alive than dead to the Vilnarians, for both information, and as a hostage."

My frown deepened. "But he has absolutely no idea what's going on with Sir Fern, Sadie, and the attempted execution…"

"And that's for the best."

I looked to Duke Gladik.

The duke shook his head. "Sir Kay is correct. It might be best to keep the ambassador unaware of Sir Ferdinand's treachery—at least for now. I've looked into Miss Sadie's whereabouts—"

"You have?" I placed my hands on either side of my plate on the table. "Where is she? Is she all right?"

"She is indeed alive."

Relief flooded through me, and I slumped back against my chair. "Good. I…I'm really glad."

"Your relief may be a tad premature, Miss Amelia…" Duke Gladik warned.

"What do you mean?"

"He means that Sadie is in even more danger than she was before," Kay scowled, his dark eyes filled with frustration.

I glanced between Kay and the duke as worry gnawed at my stomach again. "You think they'll harm her?"

"If Mr. Dourain doesn't cooperate, then yes," Kay said. "They most definitely will."

I stared down at my lap, rubbing my thumb over my knuckles. "He will," I said, more for my own benefit than for the others. "Mr. Dourain would never let anything happen to Sadie."

"Mr. Dourain is here on behalf of the Council of Law to stop a war." Kay shook his head. "He can't afford to let personal feelings get in the way of duty."

I stared at Kay in disbelief. "But Sadie is his daughter!"

"Yes, she is. But Mr. Dourain is not the type of man who will sacrifice the many for the sake of the one. He may choose Myarna over Sadie."

My nails dug into the palms of my hands as I clenched them. As their only child, Sadie meant everything to Mr. and Mrs. Dourain. But Kay did have a good point. If Mr. Dourain was faced with the choice to either lose his daughter or lose the lives of many Myarnans...

"Then...we have to rescue her now," I said quietly. "Before he's forced to make that choice."

Kay shook his head. "We can't. Not yet... If we attempt to rescue her but fail, then I have no doubt that she'll be killed."

"Then what can we do?"

Kay stared down at his plate. Duke Gladik sipped his tea. Ivan shoved a spoonful of porridge into his mouth, and Francis buttered a piece of toast, but no one spoke. None of them had any answers for me. There were no solutions—or at least, none that they were willing to share.

Ivan swallowed his porridge, then glanced between Kay

and Duke Gladik. "Not to ruin this gloomy mood or anything, but Millie asked a good question. What's next? Got any updates? Wanna let us in on your plans?"

The duke hesitated. "I'm afraid I still have nothing to report to you—though my messenger did leave this morning to deliver a note to the empress dowager. I believe that now is the perfect time to attempt to contact her as most of the palace will be focused on monitoring the emperor and the ambassador."

"I see…that's good." I managed a smile. "As long as Marta gets a message, I know she'll help us."

Ivan's spoon scraped against his bowl as he scooped up another spoonful of porridge, and Francis finished buttering his toast and placed his knife down beside his plate. I looked at Kay, then the duke. Both men had dark circles around their eyes, and their faces were pale.

Kay had Sadie to worry about—and whatever secret plans he was determined to keep from the rest of us. But Duke Gladik had an entire region of the city to manage—on top of all his investigations and evidence gathering. Choosing to assist us had led to being named a traitor, and he was still recovering from the attempted assassination. Between all of that and losing Tristan, Duke Gladik carried a burden heavier than a wagon full of lead.

I wasn't capable of helping Duke Gladik, and Kay would never let me help him. But at some point, I would change that. Somehow, I'd find a way to help solve our problems.

Eight

A knock at my door cut through my sleepy haze. I bolted upright, wide-awake and alert. My hand immediately slipped beneath my pillow, where I had placed the dagger Duke Gladik had given me for protection.

Taking the dagger, I shoved some slippers onto my feet and stepped over to the door, listening for any movement on the other side.

I reached my free hand out, carefully grabbing the door-knob as I stepped into a good fighting stance. Then, I twisted the knob and yanked the door open, ready to face whatever foe stood on the other side.

My foe had blond hair and blue eyes that nearly popped out of their sockets upon seeing the weapon I brandished.

"Miss Amelia!"

I froze, then let out a deep breath, lowering my dagger. "Oh, Francis... I'm sorry... I thought there might have been more assassins..."

Francis clutched his chest and shook his head. "Luckily no… But come, we'll meet the others in the parlor."

Francis opened the door to the parlor for me and I stepped inside. My gaze drifted around the room. Nearly everyone sat in their usual places, but this time, another figure sat on the piano bench, wearing a dark cloak. The figure reached up and uncovered herself as she looked at me.

My mouth dropped open. "Marta…?"

"Amelia, dear, I'm so glad to see you!" The empress dowager got up and stepped over, pulling me into a tight hug. She drew back to look at me. "I was so worried…when I heard the news I was absolutely devastated. Kyvir was as well… In fact, he still is."

I searched the empress dowager's face. "News? Which news?"

"The news that you and the others had died on your way to Ivanyar."

My mind returned to the conversation I'd had with the others two days ago. "Then…Kyvir really thinks I'm dead?"

Marta nodded. "Everyone did. We were told that the Myarnan assassins had succeeded in killing you shortly after you left the city."

"Then…that's why he never showed up when we were thrown in prison, or when we were nearly executed."

Marta stared at me. "Nearly exe—what? Oh, you poor

dear! I wish I had known—I never would have allowed that to happen." She looked around. "How did all of you manage to escape?"

"It was my doing, Empress Dowager," Duke Gladik said. "I could not sit idly by and let Miss Amelia and the others die for crimes they hadn't committed."

Marta held up a finger, arching an eyebrow. "Wait one moment, please...I think we need to start over from the beginning, Duke. When I first received a message requesting that I come here and tell no one, I was nearly convinced that it was a trap of sorts. But your family's seal convinced me otherwise. What exactly is happening here?"

"It's Sir Fern," I said. "He's told everyone that we murdered the real ambassadors, and he tried to have us executed for it."

Marta's eyes widened and her face grew pale. She smacked a hand over her mouth, then looked away.

"Shall we sit down before continuing this conversation, Empress Dowager?" Duke Gladik suggested quietly. "This may take some time..."

Marta straightened. She let out a shuddering breath. "I—of course," she said softly.

"I see...then the snake has finally shed his skin and revealed his true nature." Marta pressed her lips into a firm line. Anger burned in her eyes, then she sighed. "Before the late

emperor died, Sir Ferdinand assisted him with all his north-
ward expansion preparations. It doesn't surprise me that he
would want to finish what the late emperor started."

"Do you think he plans to steal the throne?" I asked.

"No," Marta said. "If that was what he wanted, he
would have done so months ago, before my son's coronation. It appears that he's chosen to manipulate Kyvir into
taking action instead."

My chest tightened. "Is…Kyvir in any danger?"

"I'm afraid that he might be. If Sir Ferdinand fails to control Kyvir, then he may change his mind about allowing him to
keep the throne." She shook her head. "Tricking Kyvir into be-
lieving you were dead was especially cruel. Ever since he heard
the news, my son has been distant and despondent. I've tried to
be there for him—to comfort him—but all he's wanted is to be
left alone. According to the servants he rarely eats, hasn't been
sleeping well, and only attends necessary meetings."

My breath caught in my throat. "He…was truly so upset?"

Marta nodded. She smiled, but sorrow lingered in her
eyes. "He cares for you, Amelia. More than even I realized."

My face grew hot and my heart jumped like a fish out of
water. I suddenly had the urge to squeal like a little girl. My
experience with men, for the most part, was limited to helping
them find books at the library.

Unlike Sadie, I had trouble distinguishing whether or
not a man admired me, and I had no idea what to do if one
did admire me. But if Kyvir really did care for me, then perhaps there was a chance that we—I shook my head, snap-

ping myself out of my thoughts. Now wasn't the time to think of that. Not while Sir Fern was out there trying to start wars and murder innocent people. I grit my teeth as anger surged through my veins. "We have to tell him…we have to let Kyvir know that I'm alive—and warn him about Sir Fern before it's too late."

Marta nodded. "I agree. Seeing as you chose to contact me, I'm guessing that you haven't been very successful in reaching out to my son on your own?"

"That's correct," the duke said. "I'm sorry to say that all our efforts thus far have proved fruitless, and…have even resulted in a casualty. That is why we've deemed it necessary to contact you."

Marta let out a deep breath. "I will see to it that my son learns the truth about Sir Ferdinand's plans. As long as I live, I won't allow Sir Ferdinand to succeed."

At Marta's words, a weight as heavy as a lead statue lifted off my chest, and relief washed over me. "Thank you, Marta… Do you think that stopping Sir Fern will be enough to stop the war?"

Marta frowned. "I would like to believe so, but I don't believe it would be wise to make any hasty assumptions in that area. Sir Ferdinand is not the only one who is pushing for war, and he's already managed to sway many citizens to his side by claiming that Myarna was behind the murder of the Ivanyaran ambassadors."

My shoulders suddenly felt heavy again, as if the lead statue had returned. The war hadn't even begun and yet it already felt like we had lost so much. The ambassadors and Tristan were dead, Sadie could be harmed at any moment, and Leon…Leon had nearly died by the hands of assassins. If war really did start, there would be no end to the pain and loss—for everyone. I sighed, then looked up at Marta. "Well, either way, we have to try."

She gave me a feeble smile. "Indeed, you must. Just as I did when I was around your age." She placed her hand over mine. "I simply hope that your story will end in a far happier manner than mine did."

"Marta…"

She smiled. "Now, now… Let's not dwell on the past. Even though I didn't succeed in keeping my homeland safe from Vilnaria's invasion, I'm grateful for what I *did* manage to accomplish, and you should be as well—no matter what happens."

"I haven't done very much…" I shook my head. "Most of my actions have only made things worse."

"And yet you haven't given u—"

"But I tried to!" I burst out, shutting my eyes and clapping my hands over my ears as all the anger, guilt, and frustration bottled up inside me escaped.

But just as quickly as the emotions appeared, they fled. I lowered my hands and opened my eyes, freezing. Marta, Duke Gladik, Kay, Ivan, and Francis—all of them were staring at me with wide eyes. I slid down in my seat as my face grew hot with embarrassment. "I…I'm sorry…I didn't mean to yell…"

Marta studied my face for a moment, then turned to look at the others. "Would you gentlemen please excuse us for a moment?"

Duke Gladik shot to his feet. "Of course." He bowed deeply then turned.

I stared down at my lap as he and the other men left the room.

"You really do remind me a lot of myself when I was your age, Amelia," Marta said. "And that's why I feel that you're more than capable of getting through this."

I brushed a few loose strands of hair behind my ear and blinked back a few tears that threatened to fall. "Well…I'm not so sure about that," I admitted. "I never wanted to be involved in any of this. And I wouldn't have been if I wasn't so…so cowardly and prideful. That day in the forest when I followed Leon instead of turning around was one of the biggest mistakes I ever made. When I was sitting alone in that horrid dungeon cell, waiting to be executed, I realized something. I've always thought of myself as the voice of reason— Leon's conscience, or at least the calm to his insanity... But the truth is, I've never made more than half-hearted, feeble efforts to stop him or change his mind. Instead of actually standing strong and fighting against his ridiculous schemes, I'd say just enough to absolve myself from any guilt. Just enough so I could say that I *tried* to stop Leon…and then blame him for any trouble that he or I got into. I convinced myself that if I did—or at least tried to do—everything right, then *I* at least would be blameless, and *I* could avoid ever getting into any real trouble. But that doesn't work in this situation… There *is* no 'right' anymore. There aren't any clear answers, rules, or even guidelines for me to follow. And now, Leon isn't even around for me to blame…"

Marta nodded. "You're right… There are no clear answers or guidelines. And that's exactly why it's up to you to create your own."

I looked at Marta, then sighed. "I wouldn't even know where to begin… And at this point I'm almost convinced that there *is* no such thing as right or wrong—as long as you have any type of authority."

Marta tilted her head to the side. "Do you really mean that?"

"No," I admitted. "But it's just so frustrating! Why is it that men like Sir Fern are able to get away with harming innocent people and manipulating them for their own self-interests, while men like Duke Gladik are hunted down and branded as traitors?"

Marta's hazel eyes filled with determination. "Sir Ferdinand hasn't gotten away with anything. In the end, there will be justice—I'll make sure of it."

I pursed my lips. "But…what about Kyvir? Will he be all right when he learns the truth about Sir Fern?"

Marta sighed. "I raised my son to be nothing like his father… As a result, he has a soft heart that is prone to injury. This will certainly cause him pain."

I lowered my head, my heart already aching for Kyvir.

Marta watched me. "As his mother, I feared that exposing Kyvir to the realities of the royal court and the machinations of the nobility too soon would cause him to become jaded and hardened… But now I see that my fears have done more harm than help. I should have taken a more proactive stance in guiding Kyvir as he ascended to the throne, but I didn't wish for him to become too dependent on my assistance. And since he was still lacking in confidence and knowledge, he relied on Sir Ferdinand for the advice that *I* should have been providing as his mother and adviser." Marta shook her head. "As a result, Kyvir was insufficiently prepared to deal with a situation of this magnitude."

"You…can help him now."

Marta let out a deep breath, then smiled at me. "Indeed… That's what I plan to do. I fully intend to take responsibility for my own part in this mess." She paused, looking me up and down. "And I hope I can still rely on you to help my son in the future as well, Amelia. There is a lot that the two of you must learn, but I still believe that you would be a good match for each other."

My face grew hot. "Even after all the mistakes I've made?"

"Even empresses make mistakes, dear. Wearing a crown doesn't make you competent."

I met Marta's gaze. Her words left me feeling warm and hopeful.

She took my hands in hers and squeezed them. "I know you're frightened, dear, but this isn't the end… Just the beginning. And once Sir Ferdinand has been dealt with, and peace is restored, I will teach you everything you need to know. You, and Kyvir."

"Thank you, Marta."

"Of course, dear." Marta's hazel eyes practically sparkled as she looked at me. "Anything for my future daughter-in-law…"

I blushed. "We're still not anywhere close to being engaged yet…"

"Have no fear, Amelia. That's something I'll make sure Kyvir remedies after we've taken care of our little snake infestation." She winked.

My blush deepened.

Marta chuckled. "All right, I'm done teasing you…for now. I believe we've kept the gentlemen waiting for long enough. Let's go find them, shall we?"

Duke Gladik, Ivan, and Francis stood in the hallway, deep in what sounded like an argument when Marta and I stepped out of the room. Upon seeing us, the duke straightened his back. He looked between us. "Has…everything been resolved?"

Marta smiled. "Indeed. Thank you for your patience. I believe I'll head back to the palace now."

The duke smiled back. "Of course. Is there anything I can do to assist you, Empress Dowager? Anything at all?"

"Yes, in fact, there is." Her smile faded. "With the amount of influence that Sir Ferdinand currently holds over the palace, it's possible that we will need additional men to support the guards who are loyal to my son in the event that Sir Ferdinand attempts to resist his arrest. It is imperative that my son be kept safe."

Duke Gladik placed a fist over his chest and bowed. "Of course. My subordinates are at your disposal."

Marta nodded. "I shall send word tomorrow. For now, all of you should gain some rest. Tomorrow will most certainly be a long day."

"Thank you, Empress Dowager."

Marta turned and engulfed me in another hug. "Sleep well, Amelia."

I smiled as I returned Marta's hug. The more time I spent with the empress dowager, the more she felt like a second mother to me. "You too, Marta."

The empress dowager pulled back to look at me, then smirked. "We'll speak more about our *earlier* topic of conversation later…"

I wasn't sure which part of our conversation she meant, but I blushed all the same. "Right…of course…"

Marta chuckled, then turned to the duke and the others, giving them an enthusiastic wave. "Until tomorrow!"

My heart soared as I watched her leave.

Nine

The next morning, I awoke to more shouting. I quickly slipped out of bed and changed into a dark-green dress before stepping into the hall. Kay was already at the end of the hallway, speaking with Duke Gladik, Francis, and a couple other guards, but Ivan joined me as I walked down the hall toward them.

"Send three squads down there. I will come myself with a fourth shortly," Duke Gladik said to the guards.

The two guards nodded and jogged past me, heading down the hallway.

"There's no need for you to go yourself, sir," Francis said. "You should still be recovering. I can handle this on my own."

The duke shook his head. "These are my tenants. *My* people. I should deal with this matter personally."

"What's happened?"

The three men turned to look at me. "Riots have broken out all over Eldnaire," the duke said.

My eyes widened. "Riots? What? Why?"

Duke Gladik exchanged a glance with Francis. The duke's face was pale and the dark circles that had been lingering around his blue eyes had grown even darker. "The empress dowager…is dead." He spoke softly, and his words didn't make sense within my mind.

Empress dowager? Dead? The only empress dowager I knew was Marta. And he wouldn't—couldn't—be speaking of her. I fixed my gaze on the duke. "What…?"

The duke sighed, his shoulders bent forward as if he carried a heavy pack. "I hardly understand it myself…" His eyes fell to the floor, and his fingers fiddled with the brass buttons on his shirt. "She was murdered sometime after leaving my estate last night. And the Myarnan ambassador has been framed as the killer."

I swayed on my feet, then stumbled backward.

Ivan caught me by the shoulders and steadied me. "Whoa there, let's find you a chair…"

I regained my balance and pulled away from the mercenary, eyes on the duke. "She can't be…we just…last night..." I could feel my heart beating faster and faster as Duke Gladik's words finally sank in. My nose and lungs couldn't agree on how to breathe, and my head felt lighter than air. "And Sir Fern wouldn't…" I gasped out. "Not Kyvir's mother…"

Duke Gladik's eyes shone with pain as he looked at me. "I'm…afraid that it's true, Miss Amelia," he said quietly. "The empress dowager has been murdered, and now I fear that…we were intentionally allowed to send a message to her."

"No…" I whispered as my vision blurred. "I can't believe it. Not Marta…"

The duke started to reach a hand out toward me, but stopped. He clenched his jaw and looked away. "I…fear I must go. With the news of the empress dowager's death, the people are in an uproar—rioting and demanding that we go to war against Myarna. I need to quell the unrest among my own tenants before the situation escalates."

"But…what are we going to do?" A couple tears rolled down my cheeks. "How can we…?"

Duke Gladik swallowed hard. "I really must go… We will have to discuss that later," he said in a low voice. "I am…so sorry, Miss Amelia." He bowed and turned, walking down the hallway with Francis.

I stood there, staring after them. I refused to believe that such a warm, lively woman could be cold and dead. I'd just seen her, just spoken to her. This had to be a cruel joke. It had to be.

For the rest of the morning, I locked myself in my room with nothing but my own thoughts to keep me company. By lunchtime, some of my sorrow had faded, growing into anger. Sir Fern was lost to all reason. The fact that he was willing to kill Kyvir's mother and frame an innocent man in pursuit of his plans astounded me. His evil knew no limits. The longer I thought, the angrier I became.

Finally, I jumped from my bed, stalked over to the door, threw it open, and burst from my room. I ran down the halls until I reached the doors to the garden. I threw those doors open as well, stepping out into the sunshine. Birds chirped and sang as they flew overhead. The sunshine and cheerful birdsong seemed rather out of place in the face of such terrible news.

I stalked down one of the garden paths, fuming. What right did the world have to be happy at such a time? Where were the dark clouds? The pouring rain? The angry thunder and flashing lightning? Why was the world normal when everything else around me wasn't? Marta was dead. Sadie's father was being given the blame. Duke Gladik had been named a traitor. Kay, Ivan, and I were under the threat of assassination, arrest, and execution. Where was the justice?

Before I knew it, the rage had faded to sorrow once again. I collapsed on the nearest bench and wept. I sat there for what felt like an eternity. Eventually my tears stopped, and all emotion was replaced by numbness.

I stared straight ahead of me, at a bed of annoyingly bright yellow flowers.

"Hey."

I glanced up as Ivan sat down next to me on the bench. I couldn't bring myself to open my mouth, let alone speak, so I gave him a tiny nod.

"I figured you wouldn't be up to training this morning, but when you are, let me know," he said. "Might be a nice way to occupy your thoughts."

I didn't answer, but Ivan didn't move. He continued to sit next to me, silent. I closed my eyes, listening to the out-of-place birdsong.

"Hey, what's he doing?"

My eyes snapped open and I turned my head to follow Ivan's gaze. Kay was walking toward the side gate. He slipped through the exit, and Ivan stood. "I've been wondering what he's been up to when he disappears every day. Maybe it's time I find out."

I looked up at him. "What?"

Ivan glanced at me. "I told you, there's something really off about that guy. I want to find out what it is. He might really be the traitor." He started walking toward the gate.

I scrambled to my feet and followed him. "You're going to leave the estate? What about the assassins?"

"If any show up, I can handle them. But with everything going on right now, I doubt that killing *me* is high on anyone's priority list. Besides, the duke did tell me to look into anyone on the estate who seemed suspicious." Ivan opened the gate and turned to me. "Are you coming?"

I blinked. "Me?"

"I don't see anyone else following me like a stray kitten, so yes, you. If you are, then we need to hurry up."

I opened my mouth, a thousand excuses on my tongue. But then I closed it, nodding before stepping through the gate. Ivan closed the gate behind us and started down the street, as if he knew exactly where to go. I followed him, looking around, but I couldn't see Kay anywhere.

"Are you sure we haven't already lost him?" I whispered.

Ivan's eyes remained glued to the pathway in front of him. "Oh, I'm sure. I know how to find people who don't want to be found. Just stay close." He picked up his pace and I had to practically jog to keep up.

He finally stopped, putting an arm out to keep me from continuing. He put a finger to his lips, then gestured to a near-by alleyway. He took a few more steps before peeking around the corner. I joined him, catching sight of Kay standing in the alleyway, speaking to a man in a red uniform—an imperial guard—and another man wearing all black, like the assassins who had attacked us on our way to Ivanyar.

My stomach twisted. Why was Kay speaking to these men? Were they all secretly spies for Myarna, or...

Ivan gently grabbed my arm, pulling me back, away from the alley. He had a grim look on his face as he turned and stalked back the way we had come. I rushed to catch up with him. He let out a string of curses under his breath, fist clenched around the hilt of the sword strapped to his waist.

"We...we couldn't hear anything that they said," I spoke up. "And Kay said he'd be working to keep Sadie safe."

"Is that so? Well, then great," Ivan snorted. "Glad to know that he didn't sell us out for absolutely no reason."

"But why would he do that?" I asked. "He's Myar-nan—a member of the Council of Law. He doesn't want war either."

"Or he's playing the whole 'if you can't stop them, join their side and save yourself' card."

The air left my lungs. I slowly shook my head, staring at the back of Ivan's head. "He...he wouldn't..."

Ivan whirled around to look at me. "He's been in *every* single meeting we've ever had, and yet for some reason he's gone at every other time of the day... How easy would it have been for him to tell the guards our plans? Like the fact that we were trying to get in touch with the emperor, or that we had sent a message to the empress dowager? I doubt that her death was a spur-of-the-moment decision. The duke is right. I bet we were allowed to get her the message on purpose so that she'd come out and expose herself without any protection."

I placed my hand firmly over my mouth. The thought that Kay could be involved in Marta's death made my stomach turn. Kay had asked me to trust him. But what if that was a mistake? Could I really trust *anyone* in this situation?

Kyvir's hazel eyes entered my mind again. If there was anyone I could trust, it was him. If only I could see him again...

Besides Kyvir, Duke Gladik was also certainly working toward peace. He never would have taken us in or saved us if he truly wanted war. And Ivan, though he was a mercenary, was also Myarnan, and seemed rather genuine about his mother and siblings. But Kay...apart from duty, why was he working for the council, and for Myarna's good? What if he wasn't? His feelings for Sadie seemed real—far too real to have been faked. But if Kay had already betrayed us once, why wouldn't he betray us again?

I swallowed hard. "What should we do?"

Ivan shook his head. "We may have to employ the same tactics as our enemy," he said in a low voice.

"Like what?"

He shrugged. "Most of our problems would be solved if this Sir Fern guy was out of the picture, right?"

My jaw dropped. "You mean—no! Absolutely not!" I hissed, glancing around.

"Why not? It's the simplest way to end this without anyone else getting hurt."

"It's wrong!"

Ivan crossed his arms. "As opposed to everything *he's* done?"

"Stooping to his level would make us just as bad as him."

"So?"

I blinked. "What do you mean?"

"Now isn't the time to think of levels, feelings, or morals, Millie." Ivan's gaze filled with determination. "This is *war* we're talking about, not a silly little game of cards or chess. You can't win against an opponent who plays dirty unless you're willing to get in the muck yourself."

"Well, I'm *not* willing," I said. "What good is winning if you lose yourself in the process?"

"I'd rather live with a bad reputation than die with a good one." Ivan shook his head. "These people want us dead. So don't think of it as murder, think of it as self-defense."

"Thinking of it differently won't change what it is."

Ivan tilted his head back and groaned. He muttered something under his breath, crossed his arms over his chest, then looked at me. "All right, fine. What's *your* idea then?"

"What?"

Ivan shrugged. "If you're going to shoot down all of my ideas, it must be because you have a bright one of your own. So, let's hear it."

I frowned. "Well…I…I don't have anything yet—"

"Yeah, I didn't think so," Ivan scoffed.

"But I will!"

Ivan cocked his head to the side. "When? Because with those troops arriving within the next few days, I'd say that time is running out, and it's running out fast."

I looked away. "I'll…figure something out."

"You have until tomorrow night. If you can't figure out how to fix this your way, then we'll just have to fix things *my* way." Ivan turned, and I watched as he walked away, frustration building up inside me.

How could anyone be so unaffected by murder? And so willing to commit one? And Kay… How could he stand there and pretend to be worried about Sadie's well-being while actively trying to harm her, her father, and her homeland? Was it all an act? Did he really care about her at all? Who was he really? Benjamin the Myarnan spy, or Kay, the *Vilnarian* spy? Where did his loyalties really lie? With the country he was born into, or with the side of the war that he thought would win?

I would just have to ask him when he returned. Ask him and find out once and for all whose side he was really on.

Ivan and I told the duke about what we had seen, and the three of us waited for hours, but Kay never returned to the manor. There were only two plausible explanations. Either Ivan was right, and Kay really had been feeding information from our meetings to Sir Fern, or Kay had gotten into some sort of trouble while in town. Neither explanation was good, and yet I desperately wished that the latter was the correct one.

Ten

*T*he next morning, I sat at the breakfast table jabbing at my food with a fork. Ivan had joined me, and the two of us were nearly finished with our food when the doors opened and Duke Gladik entered, followed by Francis. Duke Gladik's lips were pressed into a thin line, and his eyebrows were furrowed.

"Duke Gladik…has something else happened?"

The duke sighed as he and Francis took their seats. "Miss Amelia, you mentioned the other day that the emperor told you about some troops that would arrive in Eldnaire. Well, they've arrived."

I froze, fork in midair. "So soon? I thought we had at least a few more days!"

The duke shook his head. "They're here now…just in time for all the unrest of the last few days. Between the interrupted execution, the rumors surrounding Myarna and their involvement in the murder of the Ivanyaran ambassadors and now…now the empress dowager, it's the perfect opportunity for the nobles to push for action."

"That's it then." Ivan slammed his fork down on the table. "We can't wait around anymore. If we don't act now, we're not going to have another chance."

"Yes, but we have to act in the *right* way."

Ivan scoffed. "Right way? You mean asking really nicely and wishing really hard? Because none of that has worked, and now the city is crawling with soldiers. We're not going to stop an argument—let alone a war—by twiddling our thumbs and hiding away in this manor. I'm ending all of this tonight."

My eyes widened. "You can't!"

"Ending it all?" Duke Gladik narrowed his eyes at Ivan. "What are you planning?"

Ivan lifted his chin as he looked at the duke. "Are you sure you want to know?"

The duke frowned. "Likely not…"

"Marta said that Kyvir may be in danger if he continues to resist against Sir Fern's desire for war, so we have to try to contact him again," I said. "Once he finds out that Myarna had no part in the murders, and that Sir Fern is a traitor, he'll take action—I know he will! So right now, finding a way to meet with him face-to-face is our best option."

"No, it's not," Ivan argued. "If we couldn't contact him before with a message, what makes you think that we could sneak you into the palace without getting caught? And even if we did, we don't know what he'd do. We have to deal with this problem ourselves. We can't rely on the emperor of an enemy nation to save our country."

I looked to Duke Gladik, who pursed his lips. "I'm... afraid that he's right, Miss Amelia. I don't believe that speaking with the emperor will help us, but my operatives have found out—"

"Cut off the head of the snake," Ivan interrupted. "It's the only way."

"Absolutely not!" Duke Gladik said. "Enough blood has already been shed—"

"And there will only be more if we don't take this blackguard out!" Ivan's eyes flashed. "None of you seem to understand that morality doesn't win wars...determination *does*. If you're not willing to fight for what you love then you *deserve* to lose it! I wouldn't expect you to care all that much about a country that isn't yours," he turned to face me, "but you should be on my side!"

I looked away. Duke Gladik was right. Enough blood had been shed. Even if he had killed Marta, Sir Fern needed to be brought to justice in a court of law—not by the point of a blade. "It's...not about taking sides... It's about doing what's right."

"Stopping him *is* right."

"But not like that."

"Fine. If you're so determined, I'll stop trying to convince you." Ivan stood, his chair scraping against the floor. He turned and stalked out of the dining room.

I looked at the duke. "Do...you think he'll really do it?"

Duke Gladik pursed his lips. "I don't know. If he does, I'm certain there will be more chaos."

"Then…shouldn't we try to stop him?"

"I…I'm not sure."

I blinked. "You're not?"

The duke stood. "I have other important matters I must attend to, and so do the rest of my staff. Sending someone after him wouldn't be a good use of our limited time. Now, if you'll excuse me, Miss Amelia, I must go. Francis?"

Francis looked up from his meal, and after glancing at his half-finished plate one last time, he stood, joining the duke as they walked toward the dining room's exit.

I watched them go as a lump formed at the back of my throat. Perhaps Duke Gladik didn't want to stop Ivan because a small part of him wanted Ivan to succeed. I couldn't blame him if that was true. Because a small part of me also wanted him to succeed.

I gasped, straightening in my seat. What was I thinking? Yes, Sir Fern was despicable, but was it really all right for me to root for his death?

And yet…what other options were there? If Ivan was determined to kill Sir Fern, and Duke Gladik was unwilling to include me in his plans, then what could I possibly do besides sit and wait? Unless…

I stood to my feet as an idea wormed its way into my mind. It was reckless, and wild. Something I'd expect from Leon—not me, but I had to try. I couldn't give up and let Ivan have his way.

I walked down the street, away from the duke's estate, trying to remain as inconspicuous as possible. I wandered past stone townhouses, dress shops with beautiful gowns on display in the windows, restaurants, fountains, and inns on my way toward the palace.

I wore a servant's uniform and carried a basket full of apples. Perhaps not the best disguise in the world, but it was something.

The streets closer to the city square were crowded with all sorts of people. Women, men, children…but the soldiers stood out the most with their blue, beige, or brown uniforms. The soldiers in blue uniforms likely served under Duke Withermur. From reading about the history of Vilnaria, I had learned all the crests and colors of the top nobility. Marquess Dulket's soldiers were the ones in brown uniforms. His family crest had a hawk on it—which likely inspired the Dulket family's nickname, "the emperor's eyes," among the upper classes.

Which meant that the soldiers in beige belonged to Duke Carnell.

The excuse the nobles had made for bringing their men to the capital was that they needed to be properly trained. So why were all these soldiers here on the streets? Some spoke to shopkeepers and bought goods. Others fed pigeons, or spoke with each other.

I continued walking as a chill swept through my bones. None

of the soldiers would have any idea of who I was, or try to stop me, but I still couldn't help but feel uneasy. Walking through the streets alone felt dangerous, but I had no other options.

I had to find Kyvir and speak to him. I had to—

Someone grabbed my arm and yanked me backward, into a dark alleyway. Before I could scream, the cloaked individual clamped a hand over my mouth. I pulled against him, struggling to break free.

"Calm down, Lia…it's just me," the man groaned.

I froze. That voice. It was unmistakable. And it wasn't supposed to be anywhere *near* Eldnaire. The man removed his hand from my mouth and I turned as he flipped back his hood to reveal his face.

Tears sprang to my eyes. "Leon…?"

My brother grinned. "In the flesh!" He winced, putting a hand over his chest.

I took a step back, studying him. Due to my brother's height, his dark-brown cloak was only long enough to reach his knees, but it covered his broad shoulders. His wavy black hair was messy—either from wearing the hood, or simply because he had forgotten to brush it. "But…what are you doing here?" I narrowed my eyes at him. "You're supposed to be resting."

Leon shrugged. "I did rest. And now, I'm done resting. I couldn't let you take all the credit for stopping the war, now could I?" He winked.

I shook my head. "There *is* no credit to take. Things are really bad, Leon…"

"That's what I thought." Leon sobered, pressing his lips together. "I arrived in Eldnaire around the time that some of the soldiers did, so I decided to listen in and try to figure out what was going on."

"Then did you hear about the empress dowager?"

Leon frowned. "Yeah… The empress, Mr. Dourain, and a failed execution of Myarnan assassins rumored to have been caused by Duke Gladik. When I heard about that, I decided to come find the duke to see what he knew. I was just on my way to his estate when I saw you walking by."

"Listen, Leon…we don't have much time. I'm going to the palace to speak to Kyvir—"

"What?" Leon interrupted. "You've been gone for five days, and you *still* haven't spoken with him yet? What have you been doing?"

"Avoiding death, mostly…" I mumbled. "The failed execution you heard about was ours."

Leon blinked. "What?"

I explained to Leon about Sir Fern and everything else that had happened since our arrival in Eldnaire. By the time I finished, Leon was seething. "That slag! Ivan has the right idea…there's only one way to deal with men like *him*."

I shook my head. "I won't let Ivan kill him, Leon. Kyvir is the one who should deal with him."

Leon ran a hand through his hair, mussing it up even further. "I know you like the emperor and all, but I think you're putting a little too much faith in the guy. He's obviously bad at choosing who to trust."

Frustration hit me like a slap to the face. "Everyone else has already said as much, Leon. I don't need you to lecture me as well," I snapped, tightening my hold on the basket of apples.

Leon sighed. "Okay, okay, fine... So you're heading to the palace right now?"

"It's now or never. Ivan is planning to make his move tonight." I reached up and tucked a few loose strands of hair behind my ear. "Marta told me that Kyvir has been keeping to his office because he's been mourning my death—which has allowed Sir Fern to take over the palace. So I need to show Kyvir the truth... That I'm alive, and that Sir Fern has been lying to him. And after that, I need to keep him safe from Sir Fern."

Leon rubbed his chin as he looked at me. After a few seconds, he hummed, then gave me a small nod. "Okay, let's go."

I stared at Leon. "You mean...you're coming with me? But what about your injury?"

He shrugged. "My injury will be fine as long as I don't aggravate it. Besides, why wouldn't I come? You're going to need the help. I've got my sword, and thanks to my ultra-amazing powers of observation and some good old-fashioned curiosity, I know exactly how we can enter the palace without anyone noticing."

Relief flooded through me. "Thanks, Leon..."

"Don't thank me yet. You're still gonna have to find your emperor and hope that he believes you when you tell him that the man he trusts with his life is set on ruining it."

I pursed my lips, looking away. "I know…"

Leon reached out and patted my shoulder. "We're burning daylight," he said, walking toward the alleyway's exit.

I followed behind, doing my best to keep up. Nobody—Duke Gladik, Ivan, or Leon had any faith in Kyvir. All of them thought I was naive for trusting his words. But they were wrong. Even if the entire world stood against Kyvir, even if they doubted him, I wouldn't. I trusted Kyvir. I trusted him with my life.

Leon was right, getting into the palace was far easier than I expected. We went through the side gate that led into the garden—the same gate we had left from a couple weeks before. From there we navigated our way through the garden and to another side entrance, where we entered the palace.

The halls of the palace were busy with servants, nobles, guards, and soldiers scurrying to and fro. My instincts told me to hide and wait until the chaos died down, but Leon strode down the hall with confidence, forcing me to follow after him. No one stopped or questioned us. In fact, nobody even glanced at us as we walked through the crowded hallways.

Somehow, the two of us fit in perfectly just by pretending that we belonged. But as we neared Kyvir's office, the crowd thinned, and Leon pulled me aside, out of sight. We peeked around the corner. The door to Kyvir's office was at the end of the hallway, and a guard stood in front of it. I looked to Leon. "What do we do? There's a guard," I whispered.

Leon watched the guard for a moment, then nodded. "Leave him to me."

I stared at him. "What do you mean?"

"I'm going to distract him. As soon as he leaves his post, you have to make a run for it and enter the office." He glanced at me. "Got it?"

My eyes widened. "You can't! It's too dangerous."

"What other option do we have?" Leon rolled his shoulders back, then stretched his neck from side to side. "You said it yourself... We have until tonight."

I groaned, then looked my brother in the eyes. "Be careful, all right?"

"When am I ever not?" Leon grinned. He patted my shoulder, then grabbed the basket of apples from me.

I watched as he walked down the hall toward Kyvir's office. As he approached, the guard stood alert. The two of them started speaking, and I couldn't quite make out what they were saying. A few moments later, Leon dashed down the hallway, and the guard chased after him. Once they disappeared, I left my hiding place and ran as fast as my feet could carry me toward the doors to Kyvir's office. Upon reaching them, I threw the doors open and burst into the room.

It was just as I remembered it. The acrid smell of ink, the seating area with the floor-to-ceiling bookcase by the window, filled with books, figurines, vases, and wood carvings, along with a singular clock that ticked away the minutes. But none of that mattered, because straight ahead of me lay Kyvir's desk, nearly buried in stacks of books and papers. And sitting behind his desk with a blank expression on his pale face—Kyvir.

Eleven

"Kyvir!"

Kyvir stared at me, eyes wide as if he was looking at a ghost. "A...Amelia?" he gasped.

I walked toward his desk, tears springing to my eyes as I took in his appearance—his wavy curls and warm hazel eyes. He had some stubble around his mouth and along his jawline, giving him a more rugged—and no less handsome—appearance. "Yes...it's me, Kyvir," I whispered.

Kyvir slowly stood, his knees shaking beneath him as he gazed at me. "But I...you're dead."

I stopped in my tracks. Hearing the words from Kyvir's mouth made everything within me ache. "No...no, I'm not," I said quietly. "Look at me. I'm alive and well."

Kyvir stepped around his desk, keeping his eyes trained on me as if he were afraid that I'd disappear if he looked away for even a moment.

I stayed still, allowing him to approach. Soon, he was

only a couple feet away, looking down at me. His hazel eyes gazing straight down into mine sent flutters up my spine.

"Kyvir…" I smiled as a tear rolled down my cheek. "I'm so happy to see you…"

Kyvir reached out, placing his hand on my shoulder. He'd scarcely touched it when he abruptly removed his hand as if it had just burned him. "You're actually here," he whispered.

I nodded. "Yes…I am."

Kyvir wrapped his arms around me, pulling me into a tight hug. I returned the embrace, lost in the moment. After a minute, Kyvir pulled back to look at me, searching my face. "I don't understand…I was told you were dead. Sir Fern even returned the necklace I gave you." My gaze dropped from Kyvir's eyes to his neck. He wore the necklace he'd given me before I left for Ivanyar.

My shoulders stiffened. I looked up. "Kyvir, you have to listen to me… I was wrong. Wrong about everything…"

"What do you mean?"

I shook my head. "Myarna had nothing to do with the deaths of the Myarnan ambassadors. They were framed by the pro-war Vilnarian nobles. The plan this whole time was to incite conflict."

"What?" Kyvir's brow furrowed. "How can you be sure?"

"Because Sir Fern attempted to have me and the others executed three days ago."

Kyvir gaped at me. He stepped back. "Amelia…what are you saying…?"

I started twirling my hair around my index finger. My stomach was twisting and turning in knots. I had to slow down and explain everything clearly for Kyvir. I had to make him understand. "I'm saying…that upon our arrival back here at the palace three days ago, we were arrested on the spot and thrown into the dungeons," I began. "Sir Fern came to my cell later on. He spoke to me and revealed that he *wants* the war to happen—for the good of Vilnaria. And the next day he nearly succeeded in having us executed. If it weren't for Duke Gladik, I wouldn't be here now."

"I…I don't understand…" Kyvir slowly shook his head. "What you're saying, it…it doesn't make any sense…"

My heart sank. "Then…let me try again." I let out a deep breath. "It all started the day we left. Duke Gladik surprised us by demanding to travel with us, so we—"

The doors to Kyvir's office flew open to reveal Sir Fern and two red-uniformed imperial guards. My blood froze within my veins.

"Your Majesty! Are you all right? I heard that there was an intruder…" Sir Fern's eyes settled on me and lit up with surprise. "Miss Amelia, is that really you? Well, this is a miracle! When the guards reported finding an area in the woods with multiple bodies, blood, and recovered your necklace, we feared the worst…"

I glared at the red-mustached man. "Don't lie to my face! You know perfectly well that I've been alive. The guards took my necklace back when they threw all of us in the dungeons… under *your* orders!"

Sir Fern stared at me in confusion. "Are…you all right, Miss Amelia? Were you injured while fighting against the assassins that Myarna sent after you?"

"Myarna didn't send the assassins. You did!"

"Miss Amelia...I believe you are a little confused—"

"Is she?" Kyvir interrupted. "You told me that Amelia was dead. That her body had been found."

Sir Fern bowed. "I apologize, Your Majesty. I was informed that Miss Amelia's body had been located, but perhaps the guards mistook a female assassin for Miss Amelia. Since they would both be from Myarna, it would make sense that they'd look similar."

I glared up at Sir Fern, my hands shook with rage. "That's a lie!" I spat. "The assassins that attacked us on our way to Ivanyar were Vilnarian, and they were hired either by you, or one of the other nobles."

Sir Fern frowned. "Miss Amelia...what has happened? Why are you throwing false accusations at me? Have I not done everything in my power to help Emperor Kyvir foster peace?"

I whirled around to look at Kyvir. "It's all a lie, Kyvir— you can't believe a single word that he says," I warned him. "He never intended to allow your plans to establish peace to succeed."

"Now Miss Amelia, you're going too far," Sir Fern said sternly. "I'm sure that you must be worried about your homeland, but it isn't your place to interfere in Vilnarian matters."

I ignored him. "Kyvir, please...you have to believe me. Sir Fern has been deceiving you this whole time. You can't trust him!"

Kyvir's eyes filled with a mixture of confusion, fear, and doubt. "I..."

"Great men make difficult decisions," Sir Fern said. His voice unnervingly calm. "Strong emperors don't give into weakness. Miss Amelia has become your weakness, Your Majesty. Have I not stood by your side since your coronation? Have I not given everything to keep the other nobles from usurping your throne? Myarna is Miss Amelia's homeland. Even if she has nothing to do with the assassinations, do you truly believe that she'll sit quietly as we avenge your mother's death? As the emperor, you must make your decisions for the good of Vilnaria's citizens...not Myarna's."

Kyvir reached up, grabbing my necklace. He stared at it as I watched him, hardly daring to breathe. He had to know I was telling the truth. The necklace alone was proof enough. Kyvir's warm hazel eyes turned cold. He looked over at Sir Fern, then turned away. "Guards... Take Amelia to the north tower and see that she is well looked after," he commanded.

I stared at the back of Kyvir's head. My mind couldn't seem to comprehend his words. "What?"

The guards walked toward me.

I slowly shook my head. "No... Kyvir, please..."

He said nothing—not even budging an inch. The guards grabbed my arms. "Please, Kyvir, you have to listen to me—you're making a big mistake!"

The guards dragged me toward the door as Sir Fern watched, a flat look on his face. I looked back at Kyvir, but he wouldn't even turn around to face me.

"Kyvir..." I whispered as the guards took me from the room.

Twelve

*A*nd just like that, pain became my entire world. A pain so excruciating that I couldn't think about anything else. It felt like a weight had been placed on top of my head, pushing down, lower and lower with each passing second until it would finally succeed in crushing me once and for all.

Memories of the moment in Kyvir's study repeated over and over again in my mind. When he turned away from me. When he told the guards to take me away. If only Sir Fern hadn't shown up when he did. If only Kyvir had chosen to believe me instead.

No, the only one to blame in this situation was myself. I should have listened to Duke Gladik, Ivan, and Leon. Why was I so convinced that Kyvir cared for me? And even if Kyvir *did* care for me, Sir Fern was right. He had only known me for a few weeks, and I was Myarnan. Why would he ever choose me over his adviser, his country, or anything else?

The only thing there was to be grateful about was the fact

that compared to the dungeon, the tower was like a room at a nice inn. Light streamed through the large, barred glass windows. A simple cot sat in the corner of the tower room. There was even a chamber pot at the foot of the bed instead of piles of straw.

I walked over to the cot, collapsing onto it. I lay there, waiting, but the tears refused to come. I felt empty, hollow. I had nothing left to give. It seemed Ivan was right about everything. I *was* naive. Naive and foolish to think that an emperor could ever truly love me. And there really was no morally correct way to stop Sir Fern. I had been such a fool to think otherwise.

I stared up at the ceiling and sometime later, the door opened. I quickly sat up. A guard was closing the door behind him, carrying a plate of food. He turned around and I froze. "Leon…?"

Leon grinned at me as he approached. He wore an oval-shaped iron helmet over his short, wavy black hair. The red uniform of the imperial guards didn't quite fit him—his arms and torso were too long. The sleeves only went to halfway down his forearm, and the shirt didn't even reach his hips. He waggled his dark eyebrows but put a finger to his lips. "Keep your voice down. There's a guard patrolling up and down the corridor."

"But…how did you…?"

Leon shook his head, sitting down next to me on the cot. "Same way we were able to sneak in in the first place. The palace is a *mess* right now. With all the new soldiers and guards walking around, nobody knows who anybody is, or where they're not supposed to be. Now come on…let's get you out of here."

I looked away. My shoulders slumped as the tears that refused to come out earlier threatened to fall. "I…failed, Leon," I whispered. "Kyvir believes Sir Fern…not me. There's nothing more that I can do to stop the war."

Leon stared at me. "You're giving up?"

"Ivan and Duke Gladik were right. Speaking with Kyvir didn't work…"

"Well, murdering Sir Fern might not work either."

I looked up at Leon. "What do you mean?"

"I mean, don't you think that his death would be blamed on Myarna just like the empress dowager's? And this time, they'd be right. The people would see Sir Fern as a martyr."

I stood and started to pace back and forth, my boots tapping against the stone floor with each step. "Then…what can we do? Sir Fern has to be stopped somehow. But if Kyvir is on his side, then how are we supposed to do that?"

"Did you tell him that Sir Fern murdered his mother? Cause that would definitely make me turn on anyone…even if I did trust them with my life at some point."

I stopped. "I didn't get a chance to. But even if I did, I still doubt that he'd believe me. Nobody would… It sounds completely insane." I sighed, collapsing back down onto the cot before staring up at the ceiling. "It still sounds completely insane, but now—" My eyes widened, and I bolted upright. "Leon, that's it…"

Leon frowned. "What's it?"

"We have to frame Sir Fern for Marta's murder."

Leon blinked. "But isn't he already responsible for that?"

I nodded. "Yes, but *we're* the only ones who know it. We have to make sure that *everyone* finds out…"

"We don't have any proof though."

I let out a deep breath. "Neither did Sir Fern. Which is why…we'll make some. Spending time in Vilnaria has taught me that a rumor doesn't have to be true in order for it to be effective."

Leon slowly nodded. "I see what you're saying. We just need to come up with the right story. Even if we can't make everyone turn on him, we can at least damage Sir Fern's reputation to the point that people will stop trusting him so much."

I eyed my brother. "That's…not exactly what I meant…"

"But it'll work. The people care for the emperor far more than they care for Sir Fern. So if a rumor emerged that Sir Fern betrayed Emperor Kyvir and tried to kill him or something, then the very people who are up in arms and ready to go to war against Myarna right now, will be ready to go to war against Sir Fern in defense of the emperor. And if we're able to twist the rumors far enough, we may be able to get back to the truth—the fact that Sir Fern murdered the empress dowager."

I got back up and restarted my pacing. "I…suppose so… But we'll need Duke Gladik's help. Duke Gladik can shelter the emperor in case Sir Fern ends up turning on him like Marta said he might."

"Right… He can also inform all of his guards and servants to be extra attentive and alert because there's been an attempt on the emperor's life orchestrated by Sir Fern," Leon said. "Then, he can send the servants with the loosest lips off on errands, and soon enough the word will spread and the tide will turn in our favor. The very army Sir Fern had the emperor gather against Myarna will be turned against him!"

I frowned, quickening my pace. "But…what if it starts a civil war instead? What if some of the men actually like the idea of Sir Fern being in charge? What if the emperor's life will actually be in danger because the guards think that if they bring Sir Fern Kyvir's head then they'll be helping him?"

Leon stepped over and placed his hands on my shoulders, stopping me in place. "I think you're worrying a little too much now, Lia. As long as we're careful and go about things the right way, it should all turn out okay." He turned. "Now come on…I was only supposed to deliver your food and search you for any weapons, so let's get out of here before the guard on patrol realizes I still haven't come back out yet and decides to investigate."

"I'm…not coming."

Leon whipped around. "What do you mean? You can't stay here."

I ran my hand over the cot's blanket. "I *have* to stay here, Leon. If I go missing, then the guards will be searching all over for me." I let out a deep breath. "This way, no one will suspect anything."

Leon frowned. "I can't just leave you here. What if something happens to you?"

"Then I'll rely on you to avenge me."

He eyed me. "Lia…"

I looked out through one of the barred windows, admiring the city's rooftops. "There's an entire country about to get invaded, Leon," I said quietly. "A country full of innocent people. We have to stop the war before it begins…or it'll never end."

Leon glanced at the door, then looked at me. "If…you aren't going to change your mind, then here." He reached behind his back and pulled out a dagger, handing it to me. He met my gaze. "Do whatever it takes, Lia. Stay alive."

I swallowed hard, nodding. "I will. I'll do my best."

"You better…" Leon muttered. He started toward the door, then stopped, looking back at me. "You're sure about this?"

I nodded. "Go find Ivan and Duke Gladik. If anyone can make this work, it's the three of you."

"All right… Be safe, Lia."

"Amelia…"

A soft, deep voice stirred me from my sleep.

"Amelia, wake up."

I slowly opened my eyes, blinking into the light of a candle.

"Sorry…here." A hand moved in front of the open flame, reducing the brightness. I looked up at the figure standing over me and my breath caught in my throat. The reflection of candlelight danced in warm hazel eyes. "Kyvir...?" I whispered. My heart leapt—then dropped. What was he doing here? I stared up at him.

Kyvir pursed his lips, then looked away. "Amelia...I apologize for having you brought here. I...I wasn't sure what else to do. I can't afford to make Sir Fern my enemy."

I blinked. "Then...do you believe me?" I asked as I sat up.

He nodded. "The fact that you're alive and well is already proof enough that I've been lied to... I simply don't understand the extent, or Sir Fern's true intentions. If he truly wanted me to wage war against Myarna, why would he bother pretending otherwise? He's my adviser...he could have simply told me his thoughts."

"Would you have listened?"

Kyvir sighed. "No...I wouldn't have. I want peace."

"Then that's why."

"Well...he's not completely wrong," Kyvir frowned. "I can't sit idly by and do nothing... Not after they murdered my mother."

I shut my eyes as a wave of sorrow washed over me. It was still hard to accept that Marta was gone. I played with the tips of my long hair and sighed, looking away. "Myarna didn't have your mother killed, Kyvir..." I said, keeping my voice low. "The truth is, she visited us at Duke Gladik's estate the night she died—she promised to get a message to you to tell you the truth about Sir Fern and what's been going on behind your back. One of Duke Gladik's men died trying to contact you, and...I believe that the same happened to your mother.

Someone wanted to make sure that she never spoke to you. And it has to be Sir Fern or someone who works for him."

Kyvir stiffened. "But he told me—and then there was the…" He slowly shook his head. His breaths started to come out faster and faster and the warmth in his eyes turned to horror as he gazed into the candlelight. "No… Sir Fern wouldn't just—no. Absolutely not."

I swallowed hard. "Kyvir, he's currently holding a friend of mine as a political hostage. He tried to have me and the others executed. He's manipulated all of us…and you don't think he would do far worse than he already has?"

Kyvir was silent. He looked down at the floor. The flame from the candle flickered as it danced around on the wick.

"I…don't know what to do," Kyvir admitted, his voice a soft whisper. "I trusted Sir Fern…and Mother has always been here to guide me... Without them, how am I supposed to fix this?"

"I…don't know," I admitted, looking up at him. I reached out and gently took his hand. "And, even if I did, I don't think it would be my place to tell you. But here's what I *do* know. The people care for you… *I* care for you. And we all believe you are capable of ruling Vilnaria yourself. *You* are the emperor, Kyvir… Not Sir Fern."

"And yet I've let him influence all of my actions… I've taken his advice on nearly everything, and thanks to that, my mother..." Kyvir's face contorted with pain.

"Kyvir…" I whispered.

Kyvir pulled his hand from my grasp and turned away.

"I...I must go... I'm sorry, Amelia." He hurried toward the door and left the room.

I stared after him, my heart sinking faster than a ship made of stone.

Thirteen

*T*he next morning, I awoke to the sound of the door squeaking open. My eyes widened and I bolted upright as a man wearing all black entered the room. He approached, brandishing a dagger. Fear pricked at me like needles. He was already halfway across the room. If I didn't act fast, I was going to die.

I immediately reached under my pillow and pulled out the dagger Leon had given me. I stood, pointing my weapon in his direction. "Don't come any closer!" I warned.

The man hesitated, but then continued walking. He was far bigger than me, and almost certainly stronger. If we weren't in an enclosed space, Ivan would definitely suggest that I run.

I snatched the pillow from the cot and held it in front of me like a shield. It didn't seem thick enough to block a dagger entirely, but it was better than my bare hands.

I searched the room for leverage and angles, just like Ivan had taught me. I didn't need to beat this man in a fight. I just needed to stay alive and distract him long enough to get around him and to the door.

The assassin raised his dagger. From his line of sight, it looked like he was going for my shoulder. I feinted right, then stepped to the left, keeping my pillow shield up as the man struck. He fell for my feint and missed my shoulder by inches. Before he could recover, I slashed at his extended arm and managed to cut the top of his forearm. He dropped his dagger as his good hand cradled his new injury.

I darted around him and toward the door, but the man stuck his foot out. It was too late for me to dodge. My shoe hooked around the man's boot and I fell. The wind rushed out of my lungs as I slammed into the wooden floor. Out of the corner of my eye I spotted the man's boot again—headed directly for my face.

I rolled out of the way, and felt the wind from his kick. The ground was the worst place to be during a fight. I had to get up. I had to—the door to the tower opened again and another large, shadowy figure entered.

The figure darted forward, thrusting a sword straight into the assassin's stomach. My eyes widened, but no sound left my mouth as the new man pulled his sword back out and the assassin's body collapsed to the floor.

I scrambled to sit up, breathing heavily. My head and lungs rushed with adrenaline as I stared at the new man towering over me. My hand moved along the hard, wooden floor. Dagger. Where was my dagger? I needed—

"Miss Amelia, are you all right?"

I stopped. My eyes focused on the face of the hooded man. "*Kay?*" I gasped.

He removed his hood. His long dark hair was tied back as usual, drawing more attention to the scar in the center of his forehead. "I'm afraid that we don't have much time. Please, follow me." He held out his hand.

I stared at Kay, then my stare turned into a glare. I scooted back. "What? No! I know what you did! You told Sir Fern's men all of our plans!"

Kay retracted his hand as his dark eyes met mine. "I understand your anger, Miss Amelia, and I am truly sorry that it resulted in the death of the empress, but I had no other choice… Sadie's life depended on my complete cooperation."

I stared at him. "Sadie…?"

He nodded. "She's being kept in the east tower. I've been waiting for an opportunity to rescue her, and now I have it. But we need to go now." Kay held out his hand again.

I stood without taking it. "Bring me to Sadie," I said coldly.

Kay pursed his lips, lowering his hand to his side. "Of course…" He turned and walked toward the door.

I walked forward, but stopped, turning to search the ground for my dagger.

"Miss Amelia, we have to hurry!"

I opened my mouth to protest, but stopped. Kay was right. The most important thing was rescuing Sadie. I rushed after him.

I followed Kay through the corridors to the other tower. Weirdly enough, not a servant, soldier, or guard was anywhere to be seen. I opened my mouth to ask Kay what had happened, but closed it. I didn't want to hear his voice.

When we reached the east tower, Kay opened the door and we both stepped inside. It was exactly like the tower I had been placed in—a cot in one corner, a chamber pot in another, and two large, barred glass windows lighting up the tower. Relief flooded through me when I saw Sadie standing by one of the windows—bruised and a bit pale, but alive.

Sadie's eyes widened upon seeing us. "Amelia? Benjamin?"

Kay strode forward, reaching Sadie in only three steps. He wrapped his arms around her and pulled her close. My mouth dropped open as I stared. After a moment, Sadie wrapped her arms around Kay as well, sobbing into his shoulder.

My vision blurred. Sadie was alive. Kay truly cared for her. And yet, what about Marta? Was her life worth more than Sadie's? Would I have chosen Sadie's life over hers?

I would have tried to save them both. Did Kay even think to do that? Did he even care?

When Kay finally pulled away from Sadie, I walked closer.

Sadie turned to look at me, and fresh tears welled up in her dark eyes. "Lia…" She lunged forward, hugging me so tight that I gasped. "I was so worried about you," she whispered. "I…thought I'd never see you again…"

My shoulders shook as I let out a deep breath. I hugged her, swallowing hard to keep my tears from spilling out. "I was worried about you too…" I whispered back. "When I heard you scream I was terrified that some—"

"Miss Amelia, Sadie, we don't have a lot of time," Kay interrupted. His hand rested on the hilt of his sword. "I need to get both of you out of the palace now, before the fighting begins."

I looked up. "Fighting?" I pulled away from Sadie and turned to face Kay. "What fighting?"

"Earlier this morning, a rumor started spreading around the entire capital that Sir Ferdinand had something to do with the empress dowager's murder and is planning to stage a coup against the emperor."

My eyes widened. "What? Are you certain?"

Kay nodded. "Sides are already forming. Those who support the emperor, and those who support Sir Ferdinand."

I pressed my lips together. If people were choosing who they supported, and the palace was filled with guards who followed Sir Fern's commands, then Kyvir was in a lot of danger. "I have to go. I need to find Kyvir."

"It's far too dangerous, Miss Amelia." Kay frowned. "You should return to Duke Gladik's estate with us."

I shook my head. "Take Sadie there. I can't leave yet. Not until I know that Kyvir is safe."

"Well, if you're staying, then so am I," Sadie insisted.

Kay reached out and took Sadie's hand in his. "Absolutely not," he said. "I'm taking you to safety, Sadie, and I won't be changing my mind."

Sadie glared at Kay. "We can't just abandon Amelia. What if something happens to her?"

"It's all right, Sadie," I told her. The corners of my lips turned up as I watched the couple bicker. I was still angry with Kay, but it was nice to see him so worried about my best friend. "You both should go. I'll see you later."

Sadie's brow furrowed. "But Lia…"

I flashed her a quick smile, then turned toward the door. "I know. But I have to see this through… All the way to the end."

I headed to Kyvir's office, stepping out of the way of servants and guards to keep from bumping into them. Upon reaching Kyvir's office, I burst inside. Kyvir sat behind his desk, safe and sound.

"Kyvir!"

Kyvir blinked in surprise. "Amelia? What are you doing here?" He placed a folder full of documents down on his desk and stood.

"We have to go," I said, walking over to him. "It's not safe in the palace for you anymore."

"What do you mean?"

I shook my head. "Fights have started to break out. People are trying to decide who to support. You, or Sir Fern."

Kyvir's eyes widened. "What?"

"We should go to Duke Gladik's estate. You'll be safe there."

Kyvir slowly nodded. He took a step forward. "All right, I—" He stopped, frowning. "No…"

"What?"

"I'm not leaving. I am the emperor of Vilnaria." Kyvir said. His hazel eyes burned with determination. "If I left now, I wouldn't deserve that title. I won't flee simply because I'm scared. As you said before, *I* am the Emperor of Vilnaria, not Sir Fern. I will face him head on."

I opened my mouth to protest, then shut it.

"Very well…then I'll join you."

Kyvir frowned. "I'm not certain that's such a good idea— it may be dangerous." He took my hands in his. "You should return to the duke's estate. After everything is over—"

"I'm not going to leave you again," I said firmly.

Kyvir's mouth opened, but no words escaped his lips as he gazed at me. His hazel eyes filled with confusion.

I smiled up at him. "I've learned my lesson. From now on I—"

The door to Kyvir's office opened and Sir Fern entered with three imperial guards. The door swung shut behind them.

Sir Fern's lips were pressed into a firm line and his eyebrows were furrowed, but upon seeing me, his eyes narrowed. "Your Majesty, I fear that the palace is under attack." He rested his hands on his cane.

Kyvir glared at Sir Fern. "I'm aware. And I'm also aware of the cause."

"Your Majesty," Sir Fern stared at me, his gaze cold. His hold on the top of his cane tightened. "I'm not certain what Miss Amelia told you, but I can assure you that it cannot be trusted."

"But I can trust *you?* Is that what you're saying?" Kyvir snapped. "When you've been deceiving me this entire time?

And what about my mother? Do you deny your hand in her death as well?"

Sir Fern sighed. "This isn't what I wanted, Your Majesty…"

"Well, what is it that you wanted then?" Kyvir let go of my hands and took a few steps in Sir Fern's direction. "To make me look like a fool? To undermine my authority? To steal the throne? You swore your loyalty to the emperor!"

"Yes, you're correct. I did," Sir Fern said. He let out a laugh, then shifted his feet, glancing at the door. "However, *my* emperor is dead."

Kyvir turned pale. "What…?"

Sir Fern looked Kyvir up and down, then shook his head. "You are your father's son, but he was right. You're Vilnarian by blood…not by heart. That's why he asked me to help guide you after his death. To see that you continued to build his legacy."

Kyvir stiffened, his brow furrowed. "I only wanted peace," he said quietly.

"Peace requires control, Your Majesty." Sir Fern narrowed his eyes. "And control requires *force*. Pacifism topples empires faster than plague or drought." He swept a hand outward. "Would you so easily lose everything that your ancestors toiled so hard to gain?"

I glared at Sir Fern. "You had Marta *murdered*."

Sir Fern hardly spared me a glance. "I know that you've never approved of your father's actions, and that's why I chose to be a gentle hand guiding you. I didn't want to force you to take your father's path. I wanted you to come to the conclusion that his way was best on your own."

"Sir Ferdinand Richard Isaacs, you are guilty of conspiracy and treason against the emperor," Kyvir said. "Whether you've accepted it or not, *I* am the emperor now, and *I* will make the decisions that I believe will benefit Vilnaria."

Sir Fern pursed his lips. "I see...then it appears that I will have to take more severe action." He turned to the guards. "Restrain the woman and the emperor."

Kyvir stepped in front of me. He looked to the guards, his eyes narrowing. "As your emperor I command you to apprehend Sir Ferdinand."

Two of the guards walked toward us, their faces as blank as a new journal. I took a step back. I was a fool to have left the tower without retrieving my dagger.

The door to Kyvir's office burst open once more, slamming against the wall. Leon and Duke Gladik entered, and two guards with green uniforms trailed behind.

Sir Fern's imperial guards moved faster than striking cobras. One of them grabbed Kyvir, forcing his hands behind his back while another one darted toward me. I yelped as the man grabbed my wrists, holding them in an iron grip. The third guard remained at Sir Fern's side, drawing his sword from the sheath strapped to his thigh.

Upon seeing the emperor and I, the four men stopped in their tracks.

"Ah, I should have known that *you* were behind the dreadful rumors circulating about the city, Duke Gladik," Sir Fern sneered as Leon, Duke Gladik, and his men drew their weapons. "And yet I was under the impression that you wouldn't stoop to that level of lies."

The duke glared at him. "You killed the empress dowager and plotted against the emperor. There is no lie in what I revealed."

Sir Fern laughed. "Is that how you are attempting to justify your falsehoods?"

"Tell the guards to stand down," Leon said. He had changed since I last saw him. Instead of the imperial guard uniform, he wore a baggy brown shirt with the sleeves rolled up to his elbows. His raven hair still required proper brushing, but he stood straight and tall, sword in hand, pointed in Sir Fern's direction.

"If it isn't Mr. Leon…" Sir Fern's voice held more than a hint of sarcasm. "What a pleasant surprise. I heard that you had survived, but I didn't expect you to return here."

"Tell the guards to let go of my sister, and shut your mouth!" Leon snapped. He gripped the hilt of his sword so tightly that his knuckles were turning white.

"And why would I do that?" As Sir Fern spoke, three more guards entered the room, wearing red uniforms. "As you can see, I have the advanta—"

The guard restraining Emperor Kyvir howled in pain and stumbled forward as Kyvir kicked the man's kneecap.

The grip of the guard who held me loosened enough for me to wrench myself free. I threw a kick of my own at him, but he dodged, only for Kyvir to deliver a punch straight to his stomach. The man doubled over. Leon, Duke Gladik, and the guards in green clashed swords with the other imperial guards, filling the room with the clang of metal against metal.

"Amelia!"

I turned to look at Kyvir, who pointed toward his desk. "The sword I offered you before. It's beneath the desk."

My legs moved on their own accord. I crashed to my knees on the other side of the boxy furniture, peering at the dark underside of the desk. Sure enough, the black leather sheath lay on the ground just beneath the piece of furniture. I grabbed it and shot to my feet.

I unsheathed the blade and looked up. Duke Gladik had disarmed one imperial guard, holding him at sword point.

The guard Kyvir had kicked in the kneecap lay curled up on the ground, groaning, but the guard Kyvir had punched in the stomach had recovered, and was drawing his sword.

"Kyvir!" I screamed as the guard approached him. I dropped the leather sheath and dashed out from behind the desk as the guard swung at Kyvir. There wasn't enough time. Not for me to reach him, and not for Kyvir to avoid the blade swinging toward his chest.

But before the blow could hit, a man stepped between Kyvir and the blade.

Kyvir stumbled backward, off-balance. I dropped the sword as I reached him, grabbing his arms to steady him. Our eyes met, and I froze. His were wide and filled with shock.

He straightened, and the two of us turned to see the guard and the man who had gotten in his way—Sir Fern. The guard's eyes were even wider than Kyvir's. His face paler than snow. He still held the hilt of his sword, but his hands trembled. The other end—the blade—was embedded in Sir Fern's abdomen.

Sir Fern turned his head to look at Kyvir. "My…emperor…" he whispered.

The guard let go of his weapon. Sir Fern collapsed to the floor of the study.

A wave of dizziness and nausea hit me. The rest of the imperial guards had stopped fighting. Everyone stared at the fallen adviser.

I stared for as long as my stomach could stand it, then looked away, fighting to keep my last meal in my stomach where it belonged.

Sir Fern had chosen to save Kyvir.

It made no sense, and yet, somehow I understood—at least a little bit. Perhaps Sir Fern had protected Kyvir because of his promise to Kyvir's father, or perhaps he truly did care about Kyvir despite all the pain he had inflicted on him. Or maybe he had finally decided to acknowledge the truth. Kyvir was not his father, but he *was* Vilnaria's emperor. The rightful ruler, deserving of Sir Fern's respect.

One by one, the imperial guards dropped their weapons, and dropped to their knees.

The clock on Kyvir's bookshelf ticked away the seconds. I looked up at Kyvir.

He stood stone-still, staring at Sir Fern's lifeless body. His knees and hands shook.

The clock's ticking seemed to grow louder and louder with each passing second. We all stayed where we were. I wasn't even certain that I *could* move at this point.

"Duke Gladik!"

As if we had all come back to life, everyone's eyes turned toward the study door as another guard in a green uniform entered.

Duke Gladik stepped forward, toward the man. "Inform Francis and everyone you see that Sir Fern is dead," he said. "No more lives need be lost today."

The guard glanced at Sir Fern's body, then saluted the duke. "Yes sir." He turned and exited the room.

Duke Gladik turned to the rest of his men. "Escort the imperial guards to the dungeons then spread the news of Sir Fern's death."

The guards saluted the duke then turned, forcing the imperial guards to their feet.

Leon and Duke Gladik joined me and Kyvir.

"Vilnaria will never be the same after today." The duke sighed.

I looked between him and Kyvir. "Then…is it over?"

Kyvir swallowed hard, nodding. "In a way…yes, but there is still a lot to be done..." He strode toward the door.

I looked at the duke.

"We should go," he said quietly. "The emperor is right. There is more to be done."

Fourteen

The carriage bounced and rattled over the cobblestone street on our way to Duke Gladik's estate. I sat across from Francis, who had volunteered to manage the estate as Duke Gladik assisted Kyvir with restoring order to the palace. Ivan sat outside with the driver, Leon sat next to me, staring out of the carriage window, and across from Leon sat Mr. Dourain.

Duke Gladik's men had found him locked in a guest room, and the duke offered to let him stay at the estate for his own safety.

"I'm not going anywhere until you tell me where my daughter is," Mr. Dourain had protested. "I was told that she was being held here in the palace."

"She was," I told him. "But Kay—Benjamin—rescued her. I think he was planning to bring her back to the duke's estate."

I had scarcely finished speaking before Mr. Dourain insisted that we leave for the estate right away. So we had.

Exhaustion slowly ate away at my adrenaline as I leaned my shoulder against the side of the carriage. Each bump made me hit my head against the green cushioned interior with a soft thud. If it had been like the carriage we had ridden on our way from Myarna to Eldnaire, with its hard, wooden interior, I probably would have gotten a headache by this point. But as it was, my head was spinning—not aching. Sir Fern was dead. Kyvir was once again in charge. Both Sadie and Mr. Dourain were safe, and peace was within reach. And yet instead of relieved, or excited, I felt as hollow as a wooden flute.

Sir Fern's words from the day of our near execution echoed in my mind. "There is no joy in delivering justice. Only relief in knowing that the suffering of the innocent was not in vain."

He was right about the joy, but how could I be relieved when Marta, the Ivanyaran ambassadors, and several of Duke Gladik's men were dead?

My eyelids drooped as I listened to the rhythm of the carriage's wheels against the street. With no joy and no relief, only weariness remained.

When I awoke, I found myself in my guest room at the duke's estate. After changing my clothes and freshening up, I left the room and walked to the dining hall.

Mr. Dourain, Sadie, Kay, Leon, and Ivan all sat at the table, eating a late breakfast of porridge, fruit, and boiled eggs.

"Amelia!" Sadie shot to her feet, but lost her balance, falling right back onto her chair.

Both Kay and Mr. Dourain stood. "Sadie, don't move so quickly... The physician warned you against overexerting yourself," Mr. Dourain scolded.

Kay nodded, his lips pressed together and his brow furrowed. "You're still rather weak... You should rest more."

Sadie frowned. "I'm perfectly fine..." She stood once again—slower this time, smiling at me. "I'm so glad you're all right, Lia... I wanted to see you earlier but Leon said you were sleeping."

I walked closer. I smiled, but I could feel it wavering. "I suppose I was tired." I sat down next to Leon as everyone else retook their seats. "Has there been any news from the palace?"

"Not a thing," Ivan said, "though all the soldiers that arrived the other day were apparently summoned to the palace."

My eyes widened. "What? But why?"

As I spoke, Francis stepped into the dining hall. "Sorry to interrupt," he began, "but I have some news..."

I straightened in my seat, gripping the silky fabric of my skirt. "Is everything all right? What happened yesterday?"

"Once the news of Sir Fern's death spread, the nobles who were involved with the plot panicked, and a few of them managed to flee," Francis told us, "but the rest have been captured, and will stand trial for their crimes."

"And what about all the soldiers?" I asked. "Ivan said that they've all been summoned to the palace."

Francis nodded. "The emperor spoke to them. The soldiers will be sent back to their families tomorrow, and will no longer be under the command of the dukes or earls."

I stared at Francis. "Then…the war?" I breathed.

For the first time since I'd met him, Francis smiled. "There will be *no* war with Myarna."

The relief that had eluded me during the carriage ride to the duke's manor flooded over me now like a tidal wave. I laughed and couldn't stop laughing as my relief morphed into joy. Somehow, against all odds, we had done it. We had stopped a war.

Fifteen

*L*ate the next morning, we were all summoned to the palace. We gathered in the large council room.

Kyvir looked far different than he had the last time I had seen him. His hair had been combed, he had shaved, and he wore a black suit with red trim. Even the bags beneath his eyes were less noticeable. He had always been the emperor, but now it was clear. Kyvir was the emperor of Vilnaria.

He spoke with authority, none of the awkwardness or uncertainty of the past lingered.

He commanded my attention—and the attention of everyone else in the room.

"Mr. Dourain, I would like to request that you stay in Eldnaire longer so we can discuss the details of a peace treaty between our two countries."

Mr. Dourain nodded. "It would be my pleasure, Your Majesty."

Kyvir turned to look at Ivan. "Mr. Lidare, from what I

understand, you are owed a sum of money for the services that you rendered to Miss Amelia. I will pay the cost myself and ensure that you, Mr. Kay, and Miss Dourain receive safe passage back to Myarna."

Ivan's eyes gleamed as he gave Kyvir a bow. "Thank you for your generosity, Your Majesty."

Kyvir nodded, then turned his attention to Kay. "As for you, Mr. Kay—or rather, Benjamin… You have committed a number of crimes, including conspiracy to commit treason and conspiracy to commit regicide."

Kay stood completely still as Kyvir spoke, his face as expressive as a stone.

"Ordinarily you would be charged and executed, but due to the odd nature of this situation, and because you committed these crimes under duress, and to ensure the safety of Miss Sadie Dourain…I have decided to show some leniency." Kyvir lifted his chin as he continued. "I am aware that you are a member of the Council of Law, and must return to make your report to the Head Magistrate, but I must insist that you return to Vilnaria as soon as you are able to participate in the upcoming trials. If you agree to testify against the nobles involved, and resign from your current role as a spy, I will pardon you for your role in this plot."

Kay stared at Kyvir. His stony expression turned to shock.

I pressed my lips together. It was a generous offer. One I had mixed feelings about. Marta was dead, and it was partially Kay's fault. Of course, punishing him wouldn't bring Marta back, and I was certainly glad that Sadie was alive and well, but somehow it still felt wrong that Kay could walk away with minimal consequences after betraying all of us. Kyvir was the one who had lost his mother though…not me. If he believed that this sentencing was fair, then who was I to disagree?

"Benjamin? What is your decision?" Mr. Dourain asked—though from his raised eyebrow and sharp look, it looked like he was hinting that Kay only had *one* choice.

Kay swallowed hard. "I will testify…and ask the Head Magistrate to give me a different position."

Kyvir gave a curt nod. "Good."

The rest of the meeting felt like a dream. Kyvir revealed that he had given Duke Gladik the title of head imperial adviser—to replace Sir Fern.

And in similar fashion to Ivan, Kyvir offered a large sum of gold to Leon.

Then Kyvir turned his attention toward me and my heart started beating fast as his hazel eyes met mine. "And for you, Miss Amelia, in honor of your contributions to stopping the war and maintaining peace, I will award you the noble title of Lady."

I blinked. "Lady…?" I looked around at the rest of the group. "As in…it's truly a noble title?"

Kyvir smiled, nearly taking my breath away. "You've earned it, Lady Amelia."

I smiled back. Lady Amelia. I had gone from a librarian, to a fake ambassador, to a traitor, to a lady. It was like a fairy-tale—except it was real.

But before I could wrap my head around the title or what it meant, Kyvir ended the meeting by announcing that there would be a ball held at the palace the evening before Kay, Sadie, and Ivan left for Myarna.

I had to speak with Kyvir—to see him alone, but after our meeting concluded, an aide whisked him away to his next engagement.

Of course Kyvir would be busy, between trying to fix his empire and preparing for the nobles' trials, he could have very little time for anything else.

But that didn't keep me from thinking about him. How much between us meant something, and how much should I disregard? Were we friends, or something more? To take my mind from all those questions, I paid a visit to Ivan at the duke's training grounds. Ivan and Leon trained me until I could barely lift a pen—let alone a sword. After that, I spent the rest of my free time with Sadie, while Kay met and spoke about matters of state with Mr. Dourain, the duke, and the emperor.

The evening of the ball arrived, and the eight of us took two carriages from Duke Gladik's estate to the palace. I rode with Sadie, Kay, and Leon in one carriage while Duke Gladik, Mr. Dourain, Ivan, and Francis rode in the other.

"I can't believe I actually get to attend a Vilnarian dance!" Sadie squealed. Light from the setting sun shone through the window of the carriage and onto Sadie, making her olive skin glow. She wore a light pink gown with white lace trimming the short sleeves, neckline, and hem.

I smiled. Sadie was still under orders to rest and not push herself too hard, but compared to when I saw her in the palace's north tower four days before, she looked far more like her usual self. "Do you think you'll be up to dancing?"

Sadie stared at me. "Up to—" She stopped, pointing to her face. "Do you really think that I went through all the trouble of getting my makeup done and dressing up to go to a ball and not dance?"

I opened my mouth to respond but she continued.

"Absolutely not! I fully intend to dance at least three dances with Benjamin, and then I'll sit near the refreshment table and eat all the Vilnarian pastries that I can stomach."

Leon grinned. "You should try the chocolate plumb cake. It's delicious."

"Three dances might be two too many," Kay said. "We should start with one slow waltz and see how you're feeling afterward…"

"I'm feeling perfectly fine! A few little dances won't hurt me, Benny."

As Sadie and Kay argued, I looked out the window. Sadie, Kay, and Ivan would be returning home the next day, but what about me?

Kyvir hadn't offered to send me home, and he had even given me a Vilnarian title. But I couldn't continue to stay at Duke Gladik's estate forever. At the very least I had to tell Mother and Father what was happening, but how could I do that when I didn't even know myself?

Sixteen

*U*pon entering the ballroom, memories from the first day I spent in Vilnaria flooded my mind. The marble floors, gilded high ceilings, and tapestries had felt so foreign and strange to me.

I had been awed by the gold leaf decorating the walls, and the crystal chandeliers hanging from the long, golden chains. The light from those chandeliers enveloped the entire ballroom in a warm glow.

Sadie prattled on about the decor, the other guests, and their clothing as we stepped forward to the edge of the short staircase leading down to the ballroom floor. She walked arm in arm with Kay while I walked with Leon. Duke Gladik led the way and Mr. Dourain followed.

Like at the first ball, a man dressed in a red imperial uniform stood there. But this time, instead of Sir Fern, Duke Gladik gave the man our name cards. The man looked down at the note cards.

"Duke Charles Rield Von Gladik of Eldnaire!" he called as the duke descended the stairs. "Ambassador Shane Dourain of Myarna, Miss Sadie Dourain of Myarna, Mr. Benjamin Kayne of Myarna, Mr. Ivan Lidare of Myarna, Mr. Leon Robert Huld of Myarna, and Lady Amelia Lorraine Huld of Eldnaire!"

My eyes widened. My new title had just been spoken aloud for the first time for the entire ballroom to hear. Everyone's eyes were on us as we descended the small marble staircase.

"This brings back memories," Leon said in a low voice as we reached the bottom of the stairs.

"Yeah," I whispered back. "You better not get into another argument with Duke Gladik—"

"Me? Argue?" Leon scoffed. "I would never…"

Before I could respond, Sadie appeared next to me and leaned into my ear. "Why isn't anyone dancing yet?"

"Oh, that's because the emperor has to lead the first dance," I said. "The ball won't officially start until he arrives."

Sadie frowned. "But isn't he in mourning? Why would he be expected to dance at all?"

My heart ached at the reminder. At the first ball I attended, Kyvir was still mourning the death of his father. Now, he mourned his mother and Sir Fern. But as the emperor, he had a duty to his people. A duty that I finally understood. I let out a deep and straightened my back. "Vilnaria's traditions are different from ours," I told Sadie. "The emperor must lead the first dance of each ball, no matter what he might be going through, or how he may feel."

Sadie shook her head. "That's…so odd. I wonder if Vil—"

"Emperor Kyvir Velin Devar!" the announcer called out.

I whirled around. Kyvir was descending the marble staircase. He wore a black suit, black cape, and black gloves. His wavy brown locks stuck out from beneath the golden crown adorning his head—the only bit of color that he wore.

As Kyvir reached the bottom of the steps, he looked up, and his warm hazel eyes met my gaze. My breath caught in my throat. He walked toward me, his eyes still fixed on mine.

Upon reaching me, Kyvir held out his hand. "Lady Amelia, would you do me the honor of dancing with me?"

I gazed up into his hazel eyes. "Yes," I said, placing my hand in his. "I would love to, Emperor Kyvir."

Kyvir's lips twisted up into a small smile. He led me onto the dance floor as everyone watched. The musicians started to play a familiar tune, and my eyes widened. "Isn't this…?"

"The song that played during our first dance," Kyvir confirmed, bowing. "I…wanted to remember happier times this evening."

I curtsied in return, then placed one hand in his, and the other on his shoulder as he wrapped his free arm around my waist.

"I was terrified for most of that ball…" I said as we stepped forward into the waltz. "First because I was certain that I would make a fool of myself and reveal that I wasn't truly Ivanyaran, and then because Leon seemed determined to get into as much trouble as he possibly could…"

145

Kyvir laughed. He lifted our clasped hands up before pulling me into a turn. "I remember… You were so pale, I was worried that you might faint at any moment."

"I'm glad that I didn't… I'm not certain I could have survived the embarrassment."

The music changed as Kyvir spun me around. I smiled as the piano joined the mix of stringed instruments. "This was it," I said, "this was the part of the song when I finally started to feel comfortable dancing with you."

Kyvir raised an eyebrow. "Oh, I think I remember that. You closed your eyes, and I couldn't stop staring at you."

I blinked, but before I could speak, Kyvir swung me outward. I swept my hand up, then he pulled me back in. I placed my hand on his arm, looking up at him.

Step forward, back, forward, twirl. Just like the first time we danced together, the steps repeated themselves, and soon the music changed. The violin and piano faded and soft bells rang out. I smiled.

"You smiled last time too."

I looked up at Kyvir. "What?"

"You smiled, and I spoke, but then you lost your balance," he said. "I remember because it was the first genuine smile I'd seen from you…and it was beautiful."

My cheeks grew hot as I stared up at him.

The bells faded as the piano and violins returned.

Kyvir spun me around. Once, twice, and finally a third time before returning to the back and forth steps of the waltz. "Amelia…when I thought you were gone, I—" he paused as

146

he swung me out. I swept my hand up, then brought it down as he swung me back in. "When I thought you were gone, I realized something."

"What…what is it?" I whispered as the music began to wind down.

"Well," Kyvir began, "for one thing, I realized how much I enjoyed spending time with you." He wrapped his arm around my waist, dipping me backward as the music faded. My heart fluttered as I found myself gazing into Kyvir's eyes. They looked more brown than green in the warm light of the ballroom.

Lifting me back up, Kyvir let go of me. We stepped back. He bowed, and I curtsied.

"Amelia, there's something I need to speak with you about," Kyvir said.

At his words, my heart stopped fluttering and started flapping.

Kyvir offered me his arm. "Can we speak in the gardens?"

I nodded, taking his arm. "Of course…"

Crystal lamps lit the way as we walked down the garden path. The night air was cool and crisp. The stars scattered in the sky above twinkled and reflected in Kyvir's eyes.

I forced myself to look away as guilt created a lump at the back of my throat. "I…never did go to Ivanyar like I promised I would."

Kyvir stopped walking. "I'm glad you didn't." He turned

to face me, taking both of my hands in his. "Amelia... Will you stay?" he whispered.

I stared up into Kyvir's star-filled eyes.

Kyvir swallowed hard, then let out a breath. "I want you to stay here in Vilnaria...with me."

The wind blew, and several strands of my long dark hair fluttered with it, brushing my cheeks. "Kyvir...what exactly are you asking me?" I breathed.

Kyvir let go and reached out. He tucked the loose strands of hair behind my ears before taking my hands in his again. "Amelia...will you marry me?"

The world around me froze like solid ice as I gazed at Kyvir. And then my heart began hammering within my chest. I wasn't Velia, and there were no wars to stop or people to save. I could choose freely now, just as Marta had said.

Eternally yours.

Those were the words I had used when I wrote my letter to Kyvir. A letter he had never received. But if I meant those words when I first wrote them, then I most certainly meant them now as I stood before him—mere inches away.

Despite the coolness of the night air, I felt nothing but warmth inside. "Yes," I whispered.

Kyvir blinked at me. "What?"

"I said yes." I smiled up at him. "I'll marry you, Kyvir."

Kyvir's face broke out into a huge grin. He wrapped his arms around me, hugging me close, then pulled back just enough to look at me. "Amelia..." His voice was soft, but it carried the same warmth and sincerity I saw in his hazel eyes.

"Kyvir…" I whispered back.

Kyvir let go of me and reached up, cupping my cheeks with his hands. He leaned forward, pressing his lips to mine. I closed my eyes, stepping closer as I wrapped my arms around him.

Acknowledgments

Well, dear reader, we've done it! We've officially reached the end of the *Adventures in Eldnaire* trilogy.

I say "we" because of how much you, and other people like you have contributed to this series. Whether you joined my launch teams, reviewed my books and recommended them to other people, or you just randomly saw this book one day and decided to purchase it, you've played such an important role in the creation and success of this trilogy.

In fact, it's not an exaggeration for me to say that I couldn't have published these books without your support.

So, thank you!

And I'd especially like to thank the team behind *The Pearl* for all the work they've done in order to get this book through the publication process. Y'all are amazing!

I'd also like to thank my family and friends for all their prayers and encouragement. If there's one thing that God has shown me throughout the writing and publishing of this trilogy, it's that I am truly loved by the people around me.

So thanks, Mom! Thanks, Dad! And thank you to everyone else as well!

The *Adventures in Eldnaire* trilogy may be over, but thanks to you, my adventures in publishing have only just begun.

Thirzah

Author of the *Adventures in Eldnaire* trilogy, Thirzah was born in the Netherlands but grew up in Southern Maryland. She started writing at the age of fifteen, and published her first book, *The Librarian's Ruse*, at nineteen.

Thirzah writes fantasy books featuring royal intrigue, fairy tale settings, and closed-door romance.

When she's not reading or writing books, you'll find her sipping mint tea or traveling across the country. As an experienced editor and proofreader, Thirzah has worked with many writers to help them improve their work.

Learn more about Thirzah and her books on her website: thirzahwrites.com

Help other readers find books that they'll
love by leaving an honest review of this book
at Amazon.com or Goodreads.com

Want another story
by Thirzah?

Enjoy a short story by Thirzah, along with fourteen other authors, in this fun, magical collection of summer-themed short stories.

Available wherever great books are sold!

Scan for Amazon

Looking for more good, clean adventure?

Alli Prince's bestselling adventure awaits! Mechanical dragons, a crazy inventor, and lots of teen angst...yes, please!

Available wherever great books are sold!

Scan for Amazon

Ready to write like Thirzah?

Thirzah is a graduate of The Company's full-time apprenticeship. If you're ready to kick your writing into gear, learn more at:
Writers.Company

Don't stop now.
More great stories are just around the corner.

PEARLMAG.CO

New short stories, essays, and poetry posted weekly. Read and subscribe today at
PearlMag.co